Whose Eye Is
on Which Sparrow?

HARRINGTON PARK PRESS
Southern Tier Editions
Gay Men's Fiction
Jay Quinn, Executive Editor

Whose Eye Is on Which Sparrow?

Robert Taylor

Southern Tier Editions
Harrington Park Press®
An Imprint of The Haworth Press, Inc.
New York • London • Oxford

Published by

Southern Tier Editions, Harrington Park Press®, an imprint of The Haworth Press, Inc., 10 Alice Street, Binghamton, NY 13904-1580.

PUBLISHER'S NOTE
This is a work of fiction. Names, characters, places, and incidents either are the products of the author's imagination or are used fictitiously, and any resemblance to actual persons, living or dead, business establishments, events, or locales is entirely coincidental.

Cover design by Jennifer M. Gaska.

Library of Congress Cataloging-in-Publication Data

Taylor, Robert, 1940 July 22-
    Whose eye is on which sparrow? / Robert Taylor.
        p. cm.
    ISBN 1-56023-518-7 (soft)
    1. Physicians—Fiction. 2. Married people—Fiction. 3. African American singers—Fiction. 4. Coming out (Sexual orientation)—Fiction. 5. Gay men—Fiction. 6. Racism—Fiction. I. Title.
PS3570.A9516W48 2004
813'.54—dc22
                                                                                    2004000351

For Malaga and Ted,
the rocks on which I stand

I sing because I'm happy,
I sing because I'm free.
For His eye is on the sparrow,
And I know He watches me.

Old Gospel Song

Our power lies in our capacity to imagine
ourselves as other than what we are.

John Edgar Wideman, *Fatheralong*

Acknowledgments

With gratitude to Jay Quinn, for liking this story and recommending it to The Haworth Press; to Bill Palmer and everyone at Haworth, for their care and attention to me and to this book; to Tenea Johnson, for her wise and very helpful reading of the manuscript; to Constance Hunting, for once again working all the way through a story with me and giving me her always excellent advice; to Sandy Phippen, for being the wonderful writer and friend that he is; to my nephew, Anthony Taylor Rischard, for creating and tending to my Web site, as well as for his love and support; to Teresa Theophano, for her friendship and encouragement; and to Michele Karlsberg, for all she's done and continues to do.

Whose Eye Is
on Which Sparrow?

Brendan sat at his desk rubbing both temples with his fingers. He closed his eyes, kept rubbing, then opened them. His headache seemed to be better. A little. Maybe he should take something anyway. It was going to be a long, busy day.

A soft knock on his door. It opened, and his receptionist put her head in.

"Doctor Garrison? Edna says your first patient is ready."

"Thank you, Cathy. I'll be right there."

He went into the bathroom at the back of his office suite, ran a glass of water, and swallowed a Tylenol. He rubbed his temples and drank another glassful of water. He went out of the bathroom and down the hall.

The first thing he noticed about this new patient, a young black man, was how completely he filled the examining room. Not with physical size—he was of medium height and though muscular, not aggressively so. It was the force of his presence that took up so much space.

Brendan closed the door. The man smiled and held out his hand.

"Jonathan Miles," he said.

Brendan nodded and shook his hand. The man's grip was firm. He smiled again. He was handsome in a way Brendan wasn't used to noticing—full, strongly defined features, dark, dark eyes, skin a deep golden brown. *Like a very expensive tan,* Brendan thought. *A month on St. John. Or a winter's worth of visits to a tanning salon.* Brendan shook his head to dislodge these odd thoughts that were wandering in out of nowhere. It didn't work.

"Sit here, please," said Brendan.

The man sat on the end of the examining table. Brendan pulled over a metal chair and sat in front of him.

"You were referred to me by Clarice Nichols, I believe?"

"Yes," said the man. *How old, I wonder?* thought Brendan. He glanced at the chart in his hand: thirty-one. Four years younger than Brendan.

"I want to thank you, very much, for seeing me." The man was still talking. "Your receptionist said you weren't taking any new patients, till I mentioned Clarice."

"What?" said Brendan. *Pay attention,* he told himself. "Yes, that's right. We are pretty full at the moment. But I do my best with referrals from . . ." *I can't say old family friends,* he thought. "From my longtime patients."

"However it's happened, I'm very grateful."

"Not at all. What brings you here?"

"I've been having trouble urinating. It seems to be blocked somehow. Comes in spurts. Then stings a little, when it does come out."

"I see. How long has this been occurring?"

"About two weeks."

"Any blood in the urine?"

"Not that I've noticed."

"Getting better, getting worse, or about the same?"

"Worse."

Brendan wrote on the chart.

"Would you stand up please, and drop your trousers and shorts?"

He did.

Brendan lifted the gently curving penis and felt up and under the testicles. His hand trembled, just a little.

"Turn your head and cough, please."

The man turned his head to the left and coughed gently.

"Again."

He coughed again.

Nothing out of order. Brendan was relieved. He stood up.

"Turn around, please," he said.

The man's buttocks were the same golden brown as his hands and his face. *An all-over tan,* thought Brendan. He shook his head again. *Stop this, you idiot. Concentrate.*

"I need to examine your prostate," he said. "I'm sorry if it's uncomfortable."

"That's all right."

Brendan pulled latex gloves onto both hands and lubricated his right forefinger.

"Would you bend over, please?"

As he slipped his finger in between the firm round buttocks, he thought how lovely they were. Lovely? Where on earth did *that* word come from?

Concentrate, he thought. *Please. Please let me just concentrate.* He moved his finger around, feeling the shape and texture of the prostate. Smooth, not enlarged.

Brendan was, though. Enlarged. His penis was full and pressed hard against the cloth of his shorts. His face felt hot. What was happening to him? The Tylenol? He knew better than that. He slipped his finger out and turned immediately away from the young man, willing his erection to soften.

"Your prostate feels fine," he said over his shoulder. "I'd say there's no problem there. You can go ahead and get dressed."

He was glad to spend a little time in the corner of the room, his back to the young man. He removed the gloves, threw them into the waste container, washed and dried his hands, put the chart on the counter, and wrote for a while. Wrote some more. Longer than was really necessary.

When he turned, the young man—*Jonathan,* he thought, *his name is Jonathan*—was dressed and sitting again on the end of the examining table. The pressure on Brendan's trousers had subsided.

"The news is good, I think," Brendan said. "No enlargement of the prostate. Nor any irregularities there. No obstructions that I could feel in the genital area. It may be a urinary tract infection, with some swelling that's pressing on the urethra. I'll ask you to leave a urine sample with my nurse, please, so we can get it tested. If it is an infection, we'll give you an antibiotic that should clear it up. It's important that you take all of the pills, and then stop by to leave another sample so we can see how you're doing. Sound all right?"

"Yes," said Jonathan. "Thank you, Doctor." He smiled. "I'm glad Clarice sent me to you."

So am I, thought Brendan.

He nodded and went out and down the hall to Edna's room.

"We'll need a urine sample from Mr. Miles," he said, as he handed her Jonathan's chart. "Let me know what you find."

"On my way," said Edna.

Back in his office, Brendan stood beside his desk, feeling dazed. *What in heaven's name was that all about?* he thought. His face still felt hot, but his headache was gone. He stared at the painting on the wall behind his desk, dark woods and a waterfall. He kept staring.

Another knock. Cathy again.

"Mrs. Fuller's ready for you, Doctor."

"Thank you, Cathy. I'll be right out."

He heard the door click shut behind her.

When he pulled into his driveway, the big silver Cherokee was parked by the garage. *No soccer today, I guess,* he thought. He couldn't keep up with which days the kids went where.

His wife was in the kitchen talking to Marva, her indispensable right hand. Cook, housekeeper, nanny, confidant. Sandra turned when she heard him come in, smiled, and walked over to kiss him.

"You look tired, honey," she said. "Bad day?"

"Long one, certainly. I was determined to get here in time for dinner, though. Missing two nights in a row makes me feel disconnected."

She smiled again.

"I appreciate that, hon," she said. "I know you can't always make it—do I ever!—so I'm just grateful whenever you can. We all are. Aren't we, Marva?"

Marva looked up and back down.

"Besides, Marva's making lamb chops. They wouldn't have been nearly as good heated up."

"Thanks, Marva," said Brendan. "I was hoping for something hearty. And delicious."

Marva put her hands on her ample hips.

"You implying everything I make's not delicious?"

"Are you kidding? I've never tasted a single thing that wasn't wonderful. Word of honor."

"All right then, Doctor." She smiled. "You'll get your lamb chops."

Interesting, thought Brendan. Marva was *truly* black. Dark ebony. Not golden brown like Jonathan. He turned back to Sandra.

"Are the kids home?" he asked.

She laughed. "You do forget, don't you? Joshua's at Cub Scouts, and Heather's at her piano lesson. I was about to leave to go pick them up."

"I'll go," said Brendan.

"But you must be exhausted."

"A little, but this'll relax me. I promise. Besides, I like hearing about things right after they've happened. More immediate than those retellings I get around the dinner table."

Sandra laughed again. "You think so? There are days when I'd give anything for a quiet ride home."

"Well, you just stay here and be as quiet as you like. I'll be right back."

"Take the Jeep, honey. The kids like to spread out."

Long after midnight, Brendan lay awake, too agitated to sleep. For some incomprehensible reason, every time he closed his eyes, there was Jonathan. He saw, with startling clarity, his face, his smile. The size and shape of his penis. The round smoothness of his buttocks. He felt again the intense eroticism of having been inside him, even if only with a gloved finger.

Stop this! he told himself. *Think about something else.* But he didn't want to, so he kept thinking about Jonathan.

What confused him most was the suddenness with which these feelings had come over him, there in the examining room. A room he had walked into and out of, calmly, dispassionately, day after day, for more than seven years. He'd seen hundreds of unclothed bodies there—men's penises, women's breasts. None of it had been the least bit erotic. Just something to look at, to examine and evaluate. Not be attracted to. Then . . . why now? Why was this time so different? He had no idea.

He turned on one side and then the other. These frightening feelings seemed to be new, but there was a familiarity about them as well. As if somewhere back in his past . . . hazy images moved through his head without stopping. None of them would come into focus. Then one did, and he sat straight up, unnerved by the memory.

He glanced at Sandra, sleeping soundly on the far side of the king-sized bed, unconcerned and unaware. He lay back down. As he stared into the blackness of the skylight over his head, the whole thing started to unfold again in his mind.

It was at the pool out at the country club. How long ago? One July or August when he was home from medical school, so . . . eleven years? Twelve? He was in the deep end, resting his elbows along the side, facing into the pool. A young man was diving, practicing for a competition, he had thought, since he was doing the same dive over and over with what looked to Brendan like perfect form. Brendan watched him dive, swim to the far side, climb out, walk back to the board, dive, swim to the side. He saw the mass of the young man's shoulders, the molded surface of his chest, the skimpiness of his bright orange swimsuit, the rounded bulge in front.

Brendan nodded as he remembered how the bulge in his own suit had begun to grow. Immediately, he had pushed away from the side of the pool, swum to the shallower end, and stayed there in the water, looking toward the clubhouse, until his erection had softened.

Was that really the first time? The only time? It wasn't. He was sure of that. There was something earlier, before medical school, before college even, but he couldn't bring it into his head. Baseball? Summer camp? Maybe Boy Scouts. No, it was summer camp. The summer after eighth grade. He was walking through the camp late at night. Why? He must have been restless and gone out alone to look around. As he passed the shower room next to the counselors' cabin, he noticed that the door was open and the lights were on. Looking in, he saw three of the counselors standing under the water. They were laughing and joking and splashing each other. And they were beautiful.

What had kept him from remembering that? He had stood there in the dark, young and frightened, looking through the door, thinking he had never seen anything so beautiful as those three naked men. But he had forgotten that night during the passing years. To protect himself, he'd pushed that memory—and others like it, no doubt—far down out of consciousness. Until tonight, when he couldn't hide from them any longer.

He turned to look at Sandra's back, to listen to her quiet breathing. He felt a wave of love for her, for the life she had given him, for the children. None of this would ever affect them in any way. He would keep these thoughts hidden away, and enjoy them . . . Enjoy them? Oh, yes. They were pleasurable, he had to admit. But he would enjoy them in the privacy of his own mind. Let them stay there, where they belonged.

At the country club that weekend, on a cloudy, breezy late February day, Brendan saw Clarice Nichols on the far side of the buffet table. He walked around to where she was standing, balancing a plate and staring at a row of desserts. She looked up, smiled, and leaned over to kiss his cheek.

"Lovely to see you, Doctor," she said. She stood back and tilted her head. "There they are—the bluest eyes in the world. After Paul Newman's. How come you never went out to Hollywood? Gave the world a chance to see that handsome face?"

Brendan smiled.

"You do love to tease me, don't you? Hollywood indeed! I'm perfectly happy right where I am."

"Are you? No secret ambition to follow in your father's footsteps?"

"Hardly. One politician in the family is quite enough."

"Says who? That's sure not what the Kennedys thought. Or the Roosevelts. Or the Bushes and the Gores, for that matter."

"You're suggesting we start ourselves a political dynasty?"

"Why not? All you need these days, seems like, is a pretty face, lots of hair, and a name people recognize. You've got all three. In spades."

"What are you, a recruiter for the Republican Party? Or did Father ask you to sound me out?"

"Well . . . a little of both. I am still on the state committee, and the senator does let it be known, from time to time, that he wouldn't mind if you sort of followed him along to Washington. You're not absolutely opposed to the idea, are you?"

"No, not absolutely. But I'd like to actually practice medicine for a while before I head off in other directions. Speaking of which, a friend of yours came to see me this week. Said you referred him to me. Jonathan something."

"Miles. Terrific guy. I'm very fond of him."

"And you know him how?"

"We've done some singing together and just hit it off. Goodness! I hope you don't mind my having sent him to you."

"No, no. Of course not. I was pleased, in fact. That you thought of me. Is that what he does? He's a singer?"

"Not exactly. Choir director, actually. At that big AME church over on Central. Very fine choir. Excellent. He also does solo work here and there. We did the B Minor Mass together last fall, downtown with the symphony. You missed it?"

"I'm afraid I did. Just my luck."

"Well, I'm sorry you didn't get to hear Jonathan. He has a beautiful baritone voice. Stunning."

"Classically trained?"

"Oh, yes. I'm not sure where, but he's definitely studied. With some very good people. He's managed to not lose his roots in the process, I'm happy to say. Belts out a spiritual with all the soul you could ask for. Is he all right? I mean . . . he didn't say what was wrong. Just asked, since I've lived here all my life, if I knew of a good internist. I said you were the best."

Brendan smiled. "Thanks for that. He's new in town, then?"

"Fairly. Year and a half, maybe. Two years? Probably been healthy all that time and didn't need to look for a doctor."

"Probably. Yes, I think he'll be fine. How's your tennis these days?"

"Super. Thanks to you."

"No more problems with the shoulder?"

"None. And I can't tell you how delighted I am."

As he and Sandra walked into the gallery, Brendan saw that it was jammed full of people. Although he should have expected it—Arturo Vinzani was a very popular painter just now—he was still a little annoyed. He didn't like crowds much, especially not at night, in the middle of a workweek. But he was here, so he'd have to make the best of it.

Sandra was already off greeting friends, talking loudly, laughing, tossing her long shiny auburn hair, having a good time. He spoke to people as he passed. He knew almost everyone here, the penalty for still living in the town where he was born. Lots of people wanted to be seen talking to him, one of the city's prominent young doctors and the son of the state's revered senior senator. Suddenly it all seemed like a heavy load to carry around. Even so, he smiled, chatted, commented on the paintings—huge abstract masses of vivid colors. Most were overwhelming; some were disturbing. None were what Brendan would ever call beautiful, but he found them arresting.

He made it to the bar and asked for a glass of red wine. More smiles, more chat as he moved toward the other room. It was even larger than the first, and just as full. Directly across from him, on the far side of the room, was Jonathan Miles. He looked wonderful. Pale yellow shirt, open at the collar. Tweed jacket. What *was* this? Some kind of spell? He'd never in his life noticed what other men were wearing.

Jonathan turned, saw him, and smiled broadly. He excused himself from the people he was talking with and walked directly over.

"Doctor Garrison," he said. "What a pleasure to see you."

"How are you feeling?" Brendan asked.

"Much better, I'm happy to say. Almost back to normal."

"I'm glad."

11

He wasn't glad at all. He'd have preferred a chronic illness, requiring monthly examinations. Weekly.

"You like modern art, Doctor?" Jonathan asked. He was still smiling. His eyes were smiling.

"Brendan."

Jonathan smiled even more broadly.

"Hello, Brendan," he said.

The intimacy of that simple statement startled Brendan.

"Some," he said. "I like some of it. These are certainly . . . exciting."

"They are. Arturo's quite good, I think."

"You know him, then?"

"We play racquetball together sometimes. At the Y."

"Ah," said Brendan. "Who wins?"

Jonathan laughed. "I do. Usually. Do you play? Racquetball?"

"No, I don't. Alas."

"Too bad."

"I could take it up."

How on earth did *that* slip in?

"You mean it?"

"No. Not really. How would I ever find the time? To learn, I mean."

"Too busy?"

"Right at the moment, yes."

Jonathan nodded. "So I guess there's no way . . ."

"What?"

"It's silly, I suppose. I was just wishing there was a way we could get to know each other better."

"That doesn't sound silly to me at all."

"No?"

"No."

"Well . . . if you can figure a way, just let me know."

"I will."

"You've got both my numbers in your files. Home and work. Either's fine."

"I'll look them up."

"I hope so."

Sandra came toward them, slender and sexy in her low-cut black dress. She put her arm through Brendan's.

"This is a new patient of mine, Jonathan Miles," he said. "My wife, Sandra."

Jonathan smiled. "A pleasure."

"Mr. Miles," she said. "I don't mean to interrupt, darling, but we're meeting the Clarks at Romanoff's at eight fifteen."

"Of course." Brendan held out his hand. Jonathan shook it. That firm grip again.

"Nice to have seen you, Doctor," said Jonathan. "Thanks for everything."

"Not at all."

"I'm glad I had a chance to meet you, Mrs. Garrison."

"And you."

Sandra was quiet most of the way to the restaurant. Her lack of cordiality had surprised Brendan. She was usually much warmer with people, by force of habit as much as anything else. Was it because Jonathan was black? That didn't make any sense. If she'd been disturbed by that, she'd have ended up being *more* polite, not less. She couldn't suspect any of what Brendan was . . . Her radar wasn't *that* good. Was it?

5

Jonathan answered on the fourth ring.

"Brendan! What a happy surprise."

"Are you busy?"

"Only a little. Meeting in twenty minutes I'd love to skip. You?"

"Swamped. Doesn't anybody stay well any more?"

"Nope. It doesn't pay."

"Not me, certainly, so I should be grateful. Listen—I was wondering if we could . . ."

A knock at his door. Cathy's head appeared.

"Can you give me a couple of minutes?" Brendan said to her.

"Sure," she said. The door closed.

"I see what you mean," said Jonathan.

"I'd better make this quick," said Brendan. "Do you think you could meet me for lunch some day? Weekday?"

"Is that possible?"

"I'll clear out some appointments and *make* it possible. That is, if you can . . ."

"I can."

"What day is good for you?"

"Well, the beginning of the week is usually a little less hectic."

"Tuesday?"

"Next week?"

"Why not? I don't want to put it off forever."

A silence. "Nor do I," said Jonathan. "Where did you have in mind?"

"Down near you maybe? More interesting restaurants in that part of town."

"You like Indian food?"

"Love it."

"How about the Taj Mahal?"

"Perfect."

"What time is best for you?"

"I don't know . . . twelve thirty?"

"You're on. I'll make a reservation. Twelve thirty next Tuesday at the Taj Mahal."

Brendan hung up and went out to deal with Cathy and Edna and the appointment book.

Jonathan was sitting at a table when Brendan came rushing in. He stood, and they shook hands. They both sat down.

"I'm sorry I'm late," said Brendan. "I had a . . ."

"I sort of expected you might be."

"Only twenty minutes, though. Something of a miracle. What with an emergency at the office—and then the traffic."

"You don't do this often, then? Go out for lunch on a workday?"

"No. Hardly ever. Like . . . never."

Jonathan smiled. "I'm flattered."

"Good," said Brendan.

"And I refuse to feel guilty."

"Don't."

"Glass of wine?"

"That would be nice."

They ordered—shrimp curry for Jonathan, chicken biryani for Brendan. They began a tug-of-war, each trying to turn the conversation toward the other one's life. Brendan pulled harder and prevailed.

"How long have you lived here?" he asked.

"About eighteen months."

"Where were you before that?"

"Philadelphia."

"Directing a church choir?"

"Assistant to the director."

"So . . . are you religious?"

Jonathan smiled. "Enough. I grew up in the church, pretty much, surrounded by church people, and a lot of it took hold. The loving parts. How about you?"

"The same, I'd say. I've gone to Sunday school and church most every week of my life. Still do. For the sake of the kids, a lot of it, now—so they'll have the same kind of happy, secure memories I've got—but that's not all. I'd feel . . . incomplete without that part of my life."

"I know what you mean."

Their food came, and they both ordered another glass of wine. They started eating.

"You never thought about teaching music?" asked Brendan. "In a public school, maybe?"

"Thought about it, yes. But when it came right down to it, I found I . . . well, that I loved studying music, everything to do with it, but I did *not* love the few education courses I managed to struggle through."

"Where did you go to college?"

"I started out at Duke—got a scholarship there—but I transferred to the Mannes College of Music in New York my last two years."

"Are you from North Carolina?"

"South."

"You've lost your accent."

Jonathan smiled. "Most of it. That's what studying singing will do for you. Also being away for so long. It comes back quick enough when I go back home or talk to my family on the phone."

"What brought you out here to the Midwest?"

"A job offer. A good one. What else?"

"Your parents are still in South Carolina?"

"My mother is. My father died a while back. Six years this August."

"I'm sorry, Jonathan. That must have been rough."

"It was."

"Any brothers? Sisters?"

"One of each."

"Younger? Older?"

"Both older. My brother first, then my sister, then me."

"The baby."

Jonathan smiled.

"Are they musical as well," asked Brendan, "your brother and sister?"

"Oh, yes. We all sing and play the piano. Mama, too."

"Amazing."

"Why do you say that?"

"Because I can't do either one."

"You have other talents."

"Maybe. I guess I do."

"For sure you do. You cured me."

"The antibiotic cured you. I just knew what to look for."

"Sounds like a talent to me."

"Probably. But I've always wanted to sing. Of all the things there are to do, that's the one I've wanted most."

"Always?"

"Yes. Always. Every time I hear someone with a beautiful voice—opera, church solo, popular song, it doesn't matter—I think, 'I wish that could be me.' Always."

Jonathan was nodding. "I wish so, too, then."

"Will you pursue your singing?" he asked. Brendan took a sip of wine. "Try to go farther with it?"

"The 'big time,' you mean?"

"Bigger than oratorios with our symphony, yes."

"I hope so. I hope I can go farther. I don't know if it's too late for me or not."

"Are you good enough?"

Jonathan raised one eyebrow.

"Yes," he said. "Tough enough? Single-minded enough? I'm not sure. But as my daddy used to say, 'If you don't try, you don't ever find out.'"

"What did your father do?"

"He was a barber. The only 'colored' barber in town, so he worked hard all his life. Six days a week. Every week. No vacation I ever remember. He *almost* made it to retirement. He and Mama were going to travel. See the world. Every bit of it. They had lots of plans."

"What happened?"

"Heart attack. Sudden. Fifty-eight years old."

"I'm so sorry."

"Yeah."

"Did your mother work, too?"

"No. Stayed home and raised us kids. Then after we were all gone, she just kept on raising my daddy."

Brendan smiled. "Did she go see the world anyway? After he was gone?"

"No. Couldn't imagine doing it without him. She did come here last fall. That was a big deal for her. Stayed with me at my apartment for a couple of weeks. But the world? No. Too bad. She'd have loved seeing it."

"You said 'my apartment.' Does that mean you live alone?"

"Yes."

"Not married?"

"No."

"Have you ever been?"

"No."

"Ever think about it?"

Jonathan's left eyebrow went up again. A faint smile flickered around the corners of his mouth.

"Not much," he said. "No."

"You must get a lot of grief about it."

"I do."

"How do you handle that?"

"Ignore it, mostly."

"You're lucky you can do that."

The waiter came to take away their plates. "Dessert? Coffee? Tea?" he asked.

Brendan glanced at his watch.

"I've got to go," he said. "Could we have our check, please?"

The waiter took it out of his order book and laid it on the table. Brendan quickly figured half and put down a little extra for the tip.

"I'm sorry I have to rush," he said. "This has been great."

"Sure," said Jonathan, smiling. "You got to find out all about me, and I still know very little about you."

"Maybe you'll be intrigued enough to want to do this again."

"No 'maybe' about it. You say when, and I'll be here waiting."

Brendan smiled. "Gotta go," he said. "I'll be in touch."

6

When Brendan got home that night, Sandra was in the kitchen, her head in the refrigerator. He went over and leaned down to kiss her, but she turned her face away. He kissed her hair.

"Where are the kids?" he asked.

She brought a bottle of cranberry juice out of the refrigerator and closed the door.

"Marva took them up to their rooms quite a while ago," she said. "With any luck, they're already asleep."

She poured a glass of juice and set it on the breakfast table.

"I heard you turn in the driveway," she said, "so I put your dinner in the microwave. It'll be ready in a couple of minutes."

He went out to the little bathroom in the hall, peed, washed his hands and face, and came back in. Sandra took a plate out of the microwave and set it on the breakfast table beside the juice. A chicken breast, it looked like, and some rice and peas. Brendan sat down to eat. She remained standing.

"I called you after two thirty today," she said, "but you were still at lunch."

He looked up.

"Yes. Cathy told me. And?"

"You were gone for almost two hours?"

"Yes. You said not to call you back, so I didn't."

"You could have anyway, you know."

"I was busy."

"I'll bet! What on earth made you stay away so long?"

"I didn't want to just grab a bite and rush back."

"You usually do."

"I know, and I was tired of it."

"You ate alone . . . for two hours?"

"No. I met a friend."

"What friend?"

"Jonathan Miles."

She stared at him. "He's a patient you've treated . . . what? Once? Twice?"

"Once."

"So how did he get to be a friend?"

"He's an interesting man."

"There are *lots* of interesting men. Why him? Why close down the office and spend more than two hours with him?"

"I like him."

She became very still.

"You like him."

"I do."

"What did you talk about all that time?"

"Life and death . . . and music. Just back off, Sandra. I don't quiz you about everything you do or every person you've ever had lunch with. I work hard in that office hour after hour, day after day, while you flit around from bridge party to luncheon to flower show. So if I want to have lunch with an intelligent, interesting man—who is now in fact a friend—you can just back off and give me a little room."

"You want a little room? Fine. You've got it."

She went out the door. He heard her running up the stairs and, far off in the distance, a door slamming shut.

Fine, he thought. *Fine.*

He went outside, got in his car, and backed out of the driveway. The air was chilly and damp, threatening rain. He drove aimlessly for a while, then headed downtown. He stopped in front of Jonathan's apartment building and reached for his cell phone.

Jonathan answered.

"Can I come see you?" asked Brendan.

"Of course you can. When?"

"Right now? Is that all right? I'm downstairs, calling from my car."

"You bet it's all right."

"Just give me time to find a parking place."

Brendan walked up the five flights of stairs, hoping that would help calm his nerves. It didn't work. His hand was shaking as he rang the doorbell.

Jonathan opened the door. He was wearing little red silk running shorts, and a white T-shirt. Tight across the muscles of his chest. He was barefoot, and he was smiling. He closed the door. He looked so appealing, so inviting, that Brendan could think of nothing to say.

He tried anyway.

"I just . . ." What? Just what?

"So do I," said Jonathan. "So do I."

He put his arms around Brendan and leaned his head on his shoulder. Brendan hesitated, then let his arms go up and around Jonathan. He was afraid he was going to cry. He hadn't cried for years, but his eyes were full and his throat was tight. He was startled by the way Jonathan felt, so close to him. His strength, the breadth of his back, the blend of hard muscle and soft flesh.

Even more startling were the feelings inside him. Warmth. Contentment. Uncontrollable desire.

"I shouldn't be . . . ," he said near Jonathan's ear.

Jonathan moved back, put his hands on the sides of Brendan's face, and said, "Oh, yes, you should."

He pulled Brendan's face toward his and kissed Brendan's mouth, gently at first, then harder. Something in Brendan turned loose, and all his resistance crumbled. His tongue went into Jonathan's mouth. His hands went everywhere—onto Jonathan's shoulders, his back, his shorts.

Jonathan led him into the bedroom, took off his own clothes first, then Brendan's. He pulled Brendan onto the bed and kissed him again. Touching. Holding. Pleasure so intense it hurt. In Brendan's chest and in his groin. All of it fighting to get out.

"What do I . . . ?" Brendan whispered. "I mean, how do we . . . ?"

"Go where you've already been. Go in and massage my prostate."

Brendan laughed. He hadn't laughed so freely, so joyfully, for years.

Jonathan moved to the edge of the bed.

"I'll be right back," he said.

As Jonathan walked toward the bathroom, Brendan was overcome by the sheer beauty of his naked body. The muscles that rippled as he walked. He came back to the bed again, and kissed Brendan, held him. He rubbed his hardness with a cool ointment. Then Jonathan lay on his back and guided Brendan in—to where only his finger had been before—where he now was, inside this wonderful man.

It was only afterward, when his passion began to wane and his rational mind could again struggle to the surface, that fear struck him—hard.

"Oh, Jesus Christ!" he said. "What have I done?"

"Made love to me," said Jonathan. "Superbly. Why?"

"No, that's not . . . I forgot all about . . . being careful."

Jonathan leaned on his elbow.

"Did we need to be? It never occurred to me that *you* might be infected. Was I wrong?"

"No. Of course not."

"Then there isn't a problem. Neither am I."

"How do I know that?"

Jonathan stared at him. "Because I told you."

"No, I mean how do *you* know?"

"Tests. Two of them."

"When?"

"The last one was two years ago. Just before I left Philadelphia."

"You haven't had sex with another man since then?"

"I haven't had sex with *anybody* since then. Except for you, just now. Look. Here I was in a brand-new town. In the middle of a *very* conservative congregation. The object of everybody's attention. I couldn't be risking any kind of indiscretion. Still can't, if you want to know the truth. Celibacy's not my style, but . . ."

"What about . . . drugs?"

Jonathan looked at Brendan and slowly shook his head.

"You're a real piece of work, Brendan. You really are. Black man—drugs. As the night follows the day. The answer is no. I never have, and I never will. Do you want to believe me, or do you want to give me a quick urine test yourself?"

"Believe you."

They looked at each other.

"Have I ruined it?" Brendan asked.

Jonathan smiled. He put his hand on Brendan's cheek and kissed his mouth gently.

"You've got a right to be sure, Doctor," he said. "Of course you do. No. You haven't ruined it."

Brendan kissed Jonathan and settled in next to him. Jonathan rubbed his hand along Brendan's shoulder and arm. Brendan lay there for a while, completely at peace.

Soon, though, he said, "I've got to go. I've been gone too long as it is."

"How'd you ever manage it, anyway?"

Brendan sat up.

"Don't ask," he said.

"All right. Will I see you again?"

"Oh, yes. I don't know how—or when. But yes."

He leaned over to kiss Jonathan once more.

As he walked through his front door, he saw Sandra sitting in the living room in her nightgown waiting for him. She got up, came over, put her arms around him.

"I'm sorry, hon," she said. "I was being a bitch."

"Yes," he said.

"Where did you go?"

"Driving. Around."

"You didn't even finish your dinner before you left."

"I wasn't hungry."

"Are you now?"

"No."

"Well, I'm just glad you're home. I was beginning to worry."

"I wish you wouldn't."

Upstairs, Sandra kissed him good night, apologized again, rolled over to her side of the huge bed, and turned out the lamp on her bed-side table.

Thank goodness, thought Brendan. A cozy, affectionate making-up was the last thing he needed.

7 ♪

Brendan woke the next morning with a start. He looked over and saw that Sandra had already gone. He glanced at the clock on his bedside table. Six forty-one. She'd be seeing about the kids or downstairs helping Marva start breakfast. He pulled the covers up around him. He didn't need to get up for a while yet—not until seven. He reached over and clicked the alarm button off.

He could see bright blue through the skylight over his head. Last night's rain had moved on. A cloud drifted by. He stretched, closed his eyes, opened them again.

Although it seemed as if he hadn't slept at all, he knew he had—he hadn't been aware of Sandra getting up and going out. But he had also tossed and fretted. Memories of intense pleasure had been followed immediately by guilt. And regret. He hadn't actually thought *about* Jonathan, what they'd done together and what it might mean. Examining his own actions too closely wasn't his way. Throughout the night, his mind kept circling around what had happened, warily tiptoing toward it a time or two, yet reluctant somehow to come too near.

He'd have to, though, wouldn't he? Be responsible in ways he'd much rather avoid. Face it squarely. Decide what to do.

What to do. What was there to do? "Do" sounded so final. Couldn't he just drift? Have both? That and this? Maybe he could.

He hadn't been confronted with many ultimatums in his life. Most things had just fallen into his lap. Medical school, the one he wanted. Sandra. The kids. Success. An enormous house and a fancy car. Maybe this strange new desire would be the same. Maybe it would slide easily into that long chain of gifts from a benevolent . . .

No. Oh, no. It wasn't God who was tempting him in this way. Forget that.

He stretched again. Watched the sky. Felt helpless. He did know one thing for sure: all this was no whim. No passing fancy that would fade as suddenly as it had appeared. No. It was welling up from someplace deep inside him. He had no idea where it might take him.

He could just drift along and see. That *was* his way. Letting things—emotional things, not medical ones; he was good at what he did and proud of it—letting the rest of his life take its own course.

To where? If he had to choose, where would that be? What was it he wanted? Right now he wanted Jonathan. This time he thought about him head-on. No evasions. He thought about his smile, his strength, the feel of his smooth dark skin.

The effect of these thoughts was plain to see. Brendan's penis grew hard instantly. He smiled. *It,* at least, was being honest. It knew where it wanted to be.

Why? That was the mystery. Why was this happening at all? And why now? He'd been perfectly content before, hadn't he? It wasn't as if he'd become aware of some gaping hole in his life and gone out looking for a way to fill it.

He glanced at the clock. It was after seven. He had to get going and be downstairs in time to see the kids before Sandra herded them into the Jeep.

He threw back the covers and walked, naked the way he always slept, toward the bathroom, his erection swaying in front of him. That telltale advertisement of his confusion. He showered and shaved, dressed, said good-bye to Sandra and gave the kids a hug, ate the waffles Marva set in front of him.

The rest of Brendan's day went by in a blur, one patient after another. No time between. No time for lunch—not even a quick sandwich. Certainly no time to reflect. Events took over and swept him along. Jonathan did cross Brendan's mind once, briefly, around midafternoon, as he was walking toward the examining room. But inside was Esther Graham and her osteoporosis, and the thought disappeared as quickly as it had come.

He didn't get away from the office till after six. *Wouldn't you know?* he thought. He listened to the news all the way home: Trouble in Israel. Hunger in Africa. The fall elections. Two local candidates slugging it out.

As he turned into his driveway, he saw Sandra sitting on the front steps. She smiled and waved. Relieved, he waved back. She stood up and, when he stopped, walked toward the other side of his car. She looked nice in her purple parka, her hair swept back. She opened the door and got in.

"Shall we go get something to eat?" she said. "Just the two of us?"

"Fine with me," he said.

"The kids've already eaten, of course, so I thought maybe Bruno's for some spaghetti?"

"Sounds good."

Sandra chatted about her day. A phone call from her parents in Scottsdale. Her mother's arthritis was still acting up, but her father was in great spirits. He'd come in fourth in a seniors' golf tournament at the retirement village where they lived, his first big win since they'd moved out there. A note from Heather's piano teacher. A recital scheduled for the end of April. Heather was excited.

It wasn't until after they'd ordered and the waiter had brought them two glasses of merlot that Sandra looked past Brendan's shoulder and said, "I feel like such a fool."

"Why is that?"

"For being so suspicious. Of you, of all people."

She laughed. He did not.

"I just got it all wrong," she said. "Didn't I?"

Did you? he thought. He took a sip of his wine.

"Go on," he said.

"I was so *sure* I was right." She looked directly at him. "I mean, her face lights up every time she sees you. And whenever you're in the same room, you spend all your time with her, seems like."

"Her?"

"Clarice."

He was so startled he almost smiled. He struggled to hold it back and succeeded.

"Clarice?" he said.

"I know. Dumb. But there you are."

"What made you . . . ?" he asked.

"Oh . . . things. Intuition—that turned out to be totally off base."

"I . . ." *No,* he thought. *Stay out of it. Just let her keep going.*

"What really set me off was a brunch out at the club, a few week-ends ago. I saw you talking to her—for quite a long time, it seemed to me. And . . . well . . . you looked so cozy, there together. Smiling at each other. And she kept reaching out to touch your arm."

"I've known her since third grade, Sandra," he said.

"I know. I know. Just hear me out. I'm determined to get this off my chest. All of it." She looked at the table and back up at Brendan. "The longer I watched you both, the more certain I was that you were . . . well . . . then I found myself getting more and more edgy about it. So when I called and you were out for *lunch,* for heaven's sake. On a *Tuesday.* Then I was sure. You'd gone to meet her."

"But I was . . ."

"Meeting someone else. I know that now. But at the time, when you told me that bizarre story about having lunch with some patient you barely knew, I . . . I thought it was all an elaborate cover-up. You know?"

Brendan nodded. He felt the distance between them growing wider. Her instincts were right on target. It was her assumptions that were missing the mark. He could tell her. He *should* tell her. But if he did, it would be over—forever—and he wasn't ready for that.

"*Then* . . . ," she said.

The waiter put two plates of spaghetti with meat sauce in front of them. Brendan was famished. He hadn't eaten since breakfast. It smelled delicious, lots of garlic, but Sandra ignored her plate, so he did the same.

"Then, the minute I was out of the kitchen, you left. To go see her."

Brendan opened his mouth, but again decided to say nothing.

"I heard your car pull out, and I gave you enough time to get to Clarice's, and then called her."

"Oh, my God," said Brendan.

"'Oh, my God' is *right*. It was awful! 'Let me talk to Brendan,' I said. I was so *certain*. She said, 'I don't understand, Sandra. What are you suggesting?' 'I'm not suggesting anything,' I said. 'I *know* what's going on. Let me talk to Brendan.' 'He isn't here,' she said. 'Well, of course that's what you'd tell me,' I said. 'How do I know it's the truth?' 'You can ask my mother if you like,' she said. 'She's right here.'

"Sure enough, Eileen came on the phone and said, 'Sandra? What's wrong?' 'I'm making a complete idiot of myself,' I said. 'There's no one there but you and Clarice?' 'No,' she said. 'Why would there be?' 'No reason,' I said. 'Early menopause, I guess. Give me back to Clarice.' I apologized, about a hundred times, paced, tried to read, worried. Then, when I realized how late it was, I got ready for bed and went down to wait for you."

She shook her head. "I just got it all so mixed up somehow."

"Yes," said Brendan. "You did."

"Forgive me?"

Dear lord, he thought. *Forgive* her?

"Please," she said. She put her hand on his arm. "It's just that I love you so much. I love our life. The kids. Being with you. The house, even. Everything. I just don't want anything to happen to what we've got. Can you understand that?"

"Oh, yes," he said. "Of course I can."

They ate their spaghetti, drank their wine, talked again about Sandra's parents. Whether they were really happy out in Arizona or not.

On the way home, Sandra said, "So you like this Jonathan what's-his-name?"

"Miles. Yes, I do. Very much."

That at least was true.

"Well, then, by all means see him if you want to. I've got close friends I enjoy. Why shouldn't you?"

This was an opening he hadn't expected.

"Maybe I'll find out if he's free sometime this weekend," he said. "Would that be okay?"

"Of course," said Sandra. "Go right ahead."

Deceit, thought Brendan. *Flagrant, willful deceit.*

8

Back at the house, Sandra went to find Marva. Brendan left his coat and tie in their bedroom and walked down the hall to look in on the kids. Joshua was at his desk, studying. He looked up, smiled, talked a little about his homework—science, something to do with rockets and space—accepted Brendan's kiss on the top of his head, and went back to work.

Heather was in her nightgown, lying on her bed, humming as she combed the hair of one of her dolls.

"Daddy!" she squealed. "Daddy, Daddy, Daddy. Read me a story."

"Don't you want to read to me, sweetheart?"

She'd been reading for herself long before she got to first grade.

"No." She stuck out her lower lip. "I want *you* to read to *me*."

"All right. Which story?"

"'Cinderella'!"

"But you always ask for 'Cinderella.'"

"I don't care. We're only halfway through."

"*This* time."

He took the book off her shelf and sat on the bed. She snuggled up beside him. He found his place and started reading.

"'The ugly stepsisters hurried to get ready for the ball . . .'"

Sandra appeared at the door and stood there smiling at them.

"Go away, Mommy," said Heather. "Daddy's reading to *me*."

Sandra laughed. "All right," she said, and went away.

"'Cinderella, shine my shoes.' 'Cinderella, where's my dress?' 'We'll be late, Cinderella. Move along. Move along.'

"'Once they were ready for the ball, the sisters drove off in the carriage with their mother, leaving Cinderella all alone—and very unhappy.'"

As he read, he felt Heather's head growing heavier on his chest. He stopped. Her breathing was quiet and regular. He moved carefully

29

out from under her head, slipped the pillow in to take his place, and arranged the covers around her. He leaned down and kissed her cheek. He put the book back on the shelf, turned out the light, went to his room to change and then downstairs to find Sandra.

She was in the den, watching television—some sitcom he didn't recognize. A woman with a baby in her arms was yelling at a man up on a roof.

"I think I'll go to my study and read for a while," said Brendan.

"Okay," she said, waving her hand, laughing, not looking away from the TV screen.

He sat in the big leather easy chair in his study and picked up the book lying on the table next to it, a mystery he was liking quite a lot. He read part of a chapter, laid the book on his lap, and thought about Jonathan.

A little after ten, Sandra stuck her head in the door.

"I'm going up," she said. "How about you?"

"Be right there."

In bed, Sandra turned out her light and rolled over to his side. She slipped in under his arm. He'd been afraid of that. He switched off his light and put his other arm around her.

Could he do this? So soon after . . . ?

She was soft, round, familiar. Yes. He could do it.

9

Brendan left home a little early the next morning, pulled over a few blocks from his house, reached for his cell phone, and called Jonathan. When he heard Jonathan's voice—deep, resonant, warm—he felt his stomach quiver.

"I'm so glad you're still there," said Brendan. "I had no idea what time you have to leave in the morning."

"About eight fifteen. Usually. I've been wishing . . . *hoping* . . . every time the phone rang."

"I'm sorry. Yesterday was . . ."

"No, no, no. I understand. I just wanted you to know how much I was missing you."

"I can hear it in your voice, and it makes me happy."

"Good."

"Listen. Any chance I could see you sometime this weekend?"

"Are you serious?"

"It's my wife's idea. She thinks we're . . . I'll explain it all when I see you. So is it possible?"

"Depends on when you're talking about. Sunday morning's out, of course, and the early part of the afternoon."

"Yeah. Evenings are no good for me. Almost always. I need to be there for dinner with Sandra and the kids whenever I can. I like to spend time with each of them before they go to bed. But Saturday? Morning or afternoon?"

"Well, I . . ."

"Problem?"

"Sort of. This is my week to volunteer at the health clinic, down on the South Side. One Saturday a month. I could, but I hate to skip out on them with so little notice. They're really shorthanded down there. Especially on Saturdays."

"What do you do at this clinic?"

Jonathan laughed. "Administrative things. Appointments. A little bookkeeping. I'm terrific on the switchboard."

"I'm sure you are."

"But nothing medical. Don't worry. They're not *that* desperate."

"How long do you have to be there?"

"Nine to three."

"Well, why don't I come by about two thirty? Let you show me around a little. I don't know anything about this place, and I'm curious. Then, after you get off, we could spend some time together. How's that?"

"Pretty wonderful, I'd say. I'd love to show you the clinic. They do some amazing work."

Saturday afternoon was clear and sunny, warm for late March. Brendan followed Jonathan's directions into a part of town he'd never seen—except for crime reports on the evening news. The closer he got to the clinic, the more nervous the surroundings made him. He turned off Eighteenth onto South Cumberland, and there it was, a one-story building that filled half a block. He was hesitant about parking his car in such a run-down neighborhood. A Lexus convertible would be an almost irresistible temptation. He thought about driving uptown and taking a cab back down. But he was eager to see Jonathan and didn't want to use up that much time.

He found a place around the corner from the clinic, pulled in, almost pulled out again, but decided to risk it. He locked the doors with his key. The flashing lights and little beep of the remote locking system would just attract unwanted attention.

The sidewalks were littered with trash, the walls of the buildings covered with graffiti. Brendan looked around, saw no one on the street, and walked quickly toward the front door of the clinic. Inside was turmoil. People milling around or sitting on cast-off chairs and sofas. Leaning against the walls. Children screaming, running, sitting on the floor, crying, shouting.

Brendan pushed his way through as politely as he could. "Excuse me," he said. "I'm sorry. Excuse me."

At the far side of the large waiting room was a reception area—a counter with desks behind it, a couple of beat-up computer terminals. Four people were sitting there, trying vainly, so far as Brendan could see, to bring order out of this chaos. One of them was Jonathan. As always when he saw him, Brendan's throat and chest felt tight. He watched for a few minutes as Jonathan listened patiently to a very large, very black woman who was yelling at him and waving her hands.

Jonathan said something to her, shook his head, and pointed behind him. She yelled some more. Jonathan shook his head again. He glanced over and saw Brendan. A tiny smile tugged at the corners of his mouth. He held up one finger, raised his eyebrows, and turned back to the irate woman.

She yelled. Jonathan listened. She yelled. He shook his head, wrote on a piece of paper, and handed it to her. She yelled some more, but finally turned and went away. The man standing behind her pushed forward to the edge of the counter. Jonathan looked to his right and motioned with his hand. A pretty young Hispanic woman came over, bent down to listen, nodded. Jonathan stood and moved aside. She sat in the chair and looked up with a smile at the man standing in front of her.

Jonathan waved at Brendan and pointed toward the end of the counter. Brendan nodded and pushed his way in that direction, excusing himself as he went. Jonathan held out his hand, shook Brendan's, and said, "Hi."

Brendan smiled. "Hi," he said.

"A bit more crowded than your office, isn't it?"

"A bit."

"Come on back and take a look. Everything's pretty well jammed at the moment. Saturday's mostly for kids, as you can see. Checkups. Immunizations. So parents who work can bring them in. Stuff our nurses and physician's assistants can handle."

"No doctors on duty?"

"Usually, whenever we can. For backup. But not today."

Jonathan showed Brendan an emergency-care room—spotlessly clean but with equipment that was showing its age. The consulting rooms on both sides of the hall were full. Children, mostly screaming. Adults, sometimes one, sometimes two, looking concerned. A nurse or a PA, mostly young, mostly black.

"Busy place," said Brendan.

Jonathan laughed. "Always," he said.

They stopped in the hallway near the reception area.

"How did you ever get involved here, anyway?" asked Brendan.

"It goes way back. I started out being a buddy to some AIDS patients. In New York, and then Philadelphia. Friends who got sick at first. Later on, anybody who needed me. But . . . they all kept dying. So many that when I moved here, I thought I'd done that enough. Turned out I was wrong. I missed it, so when I heard about this place, I started coming here."

Brendan looked around.

"But it's not just for AIDS," he said. "Is it?"

"Oh, no. It's for the whole community. Provides free health care to those who've got no insurance. Mostly black and Hispanic, given the neighborhood."

"Free? It can't be free."

"Yes. It is."

"But who funds it? This is a big operation."

"Charities. A number of churches, mine included. Some corporations. Not many, but . . . some. A couple of well-heeled individuals. And, a good many of the doctors donate their time. A few hours a week."

"Donate?"

"Pro bono. Like the lawyers do."

"I've never heard of that."

Jonathan shrugged. "Maybe you just haven't been listening."

"Well. It is a bit out of my normal . . ."

"Frame of reference?" said Jonathan. "Like me?"

He winked.

Brendan smiled. "Yeah. Like you."

There was a sudden commotion over by the front door. Brendan could see two young black men carrying in a woman who was clearly unconscious. A small, wiry older woman beside them was shrieking,

"Git over here, somebody. Shantelle been hurt—bad. Goddamn Conroy. Hit her sump'n awful this time. Git on *over* here! She jis' barely breathin'."

Two women and a man ran out from the direction of the consulting rooms. Brendan and Jonathan followed them. The crowd parted to let them through. The two men carrying the injured woman laid her on a just-vacated couch. Brendan and the others knelt beside her.

"None of you are doctors?" asked Brendan.

"No," said one of the women.

"I am. May I examine her? There's no time to lose."

"Please. Go ahead."

He touched the woman's battered face and neck gently. He felt quickly over the rest of her body.

"Her jaw is broken, and her throat's obstructed," he said. "Wait. She's stopped breathing. We've got to get oxygen into her, fast. What's the nearest hospital?"

"Sloane Memorial."

"Damn," said Brendan. "Ten, fifteen minutes at best. Half an hour both ways. That's far too long."

He felt panic rising in him, but shoved it away.

"Call an ambulance from there anyway. For follow-up care." One of the women beside him got up and ran toward the desks. "We'll have to do something ourselves. Right away."

"Like what, Doctor?" asked the other woman.

Brendan glanced at her name tag. Betty Proctor, RN.

"A tracheostomy. It's the only way."

Her eyes grew wide.

"Have you done many of them?"

"None. I've only seen it done twice, but we have no choice."

The crowd around them was hushed, listening.

"But, Doctor," she said. "I'm not sure we're authorized to do a thing like that. We have rules and procedures we're required to follow. Permissions we're obligated to . . ."

"Rules be damned," said Brendan. "If we follow your rules, she will die." He heard a moan behind him. "Or be brain-dead, which is very much the same. All you're doing is wasting precious time. Surely you have a scalpel?"

"Of course."

"And some kind of tube we could sterilize?"

She nodded.

"Then let's get going."

The small, wiry woman grabbed Brendan's arm. Tears were sliding down her face.

"Shantelle my daughter, Doctor. Do what you gotta do to save her, hear? You hear me?"

"I'll do my best, ma'am. You can be sure of that." He was talking fast. "This man's name is Jonathan. He'll take care of you, all right?"

She nodded. Jonathan put his hand on Brendan's shoulder and squeezed.

"Okay, folks," said Brendan. "Let's get cracking. We've got work to do."

He ran to the emergency-care room, found the sink, and started scrubbing. Nurse Proctor and a male nurse came in after him. He heard them moving the bed and getting instruments out of the cabinets.

Brendan turned and held his hands up. The male nurse came quickly over and slipped gloves on them. His name tag said Doug Saunders.

"Thank you, Saunders," said Brendan.

The man smiled.

A man and a woman wheeled Shantelle in on a gurney, shifted her onto the bed, and began cutting away her bloody clothing.

"Start an IV, please, Saunders," said Brendan.

A young woman he hadn't seen before came rushing in.

"I'm one of the PAs," she said.

"And your name is . . . ?" asked Brendan.

"Ortega. Gloria Ortega."

"We're prepping for an emergency tracheostomy, Ortega." The woman nodded. "See what you can do about the bleeding, if you will. Get her as stable as you can."

"Right."

Jonathan appeared at the door with Shantelle's mother.

"There, Mrs. Benson," he said. "You see? They're doing everything they can to help her. I'm going to close the door now, so they won't be disturbed. I'd like you to sit with me while we wait. All right?"

The woman nodded, and Jonathan closed the door.

Brendan walked over to the bed.

"Okay, everybody," he said. "Let's get started."

He held out his hand.

"Scalpel."

Proctor, her hands now gloved, slapped a scalpel into his palm.

"I'm going straight through the cricothyroid membrane. That will give us direct access to the airway."

He sliced across Shantelle's neck. Blood spurted. Saunders moved in to stanch it. Brendan carefully separated her neck muscles and pushed her thyroid gland up and out of the way. Beneath were the rings of cartilage on the outer wall of her trachea.

This is it, he thought. His hands wanted to tremble, but he wouldn't let them. He heard the wail of a siren growing louder by the second. He took a deep breath and cut through two of the rings on the ex- posed trachea.

"Tube," he said.

Proctor slapped a short length of plastic tubing into his hand. Very, very carefully he pushed it into the slit he had made. He pressed on Shantelle's chest. Air flowed out of the tube. He pressed again. She gasped, pulled air in through the tube, gasped again, began to breathe. It was shallow and tentative, but she was breathing.

Brendan felt a gentle pat on his back, then another. His eyes filled with tears. The sound of the siren had stopped.

Proctor moved the skin of Shantelle's neck in tight around the tube and began taping it in place.

"Her pulse is slowing, no longer irregular," said Ortega. "Blood pressure coming back up. Nice work, Doctor."

"Thank you," said Brendan.

The door burst open, and three men rushed in.

"We're from Sloane," said one. "Got here as quick as we could."

"I've done an emergency tracheostomy. Her jaw's been broken, as you will see. They'll need to replace our tube with a proper one as soon as possible."

"Roger," said the man.

Brendan stood back and watched as they slid Shantelle onto their gurney, shifted the IV bag over to their holder, and wheeled her out through the door. He stripped off his gloves, looked around for a chair, and sat with his head in his hands.

He felt someone rubbing the back of his neck. He looked up. Jonathan was smiling down at him. He heard the siren start up again.

"Sounds like they're on their way," said Brendan. "Thank God."

"They are," said Jonathan. "With Mrs. Benson riding along, telling everyone what to do. She wanted me to thank you. 'Give that man a hug for me,' she said. 'You hear?' "

Brendan stood up. They put their arms around each other, and Brendan closed his eyes.

Yes, he thought. *Yes.*

"Just a little hug, though," Jonathan whispered. "For the time being."

Brendan nodded, and they moved apart.

"The crew from Sloane was very impressed with your work," said Jonathan.

"As were we," said Proctor. "Sorry I was so . . . you were right, of course."

"Don't give it another thought," said Brendan. "We have to be cautious. Most of the time."

He held out his hand. She shook it. He walked over to where Ortega and Saunders were standing and shook their hands as well.

"Thank you," he said. "You were a great team."

"No," said Ortega. "*We* were. A great team."

"I think I'll run on up to Sloane and see how she's doing. Ride along with me, Jonathan?"

Jonathan smiled and nodded.

"Absolutely."

10

Brendan and Jonathan walked out of the clinic into the afternoon sunshine. A breeze was blowing warmer air up from somewhere down south. Spring was on its way.

"Did you bring a car?" asked Brendan.

"No," said Jonathan. "Came on the bus, as usual. Parking's impossible in my neighborhood on the weekends, so I just leave my car there whenever I can. Besides, the bus stops right across the street—there and here. Where's your car?"

"Around the corner."

As they walked, Jonathan put his hand on Brendan's shoulder briefly, then took it away.

"You were wonderful," he said.

"Was I?"

"I should say. I loved the way you took charge. Decided what needed to be done and just swept everybody along with you."

"It was a pretty simple choice, really. That or losing her."

"Simple to make, maybe. But not to carry out. I still say you were wonderful."

"Thanks."

They turned the corner. Brendan's car was waiting there, right where he'd left it. He used his key again. This time the flash and beep would have seemed ostentatious.

Jonathan whistled.

"You travel in *style*, don't you?" he said.

Brendan laughed. "Most of the time, yes."

Inside the car, Brendan turned to look at Jonathan.

"Even a quick kiss would be dangerous, wouldn't it?" he said.

Jonathan nodded. "I'd say so. You never know who might be watching."

"I'd love it, though . . . if we could."

"So would I."

Brendan shook his head to break the spell.

"Let's go see if that young woman's all right," he said.

He turned left at the corner, off South Cumberland onto Eighteenth, then onto the freeway headed north.

"I'm dying to know how you got to come today," said Jonathan.

"By letting my wife believe a lie."

"Ah. You find that painful."

"I do. But not painful enough not to come."

"It's a complex web, isn't it?"

"Very."

"I understand your dilemma," said Jonathan. "At least I think I do. I'm not going to be the least bit helpful about it, though. I want to be with you whenever I can. However I can. It may be selfish, but I can't help that."

"Nor can I," said Brendan. "In Hollywood, they'd say, 'It's bigger than both of us.'"

Jonathan laughed. "So they would."

He was quiet for a minute, then turned to look at Brendan.

"What lie, exactly, does your wife believe?" he asked.

"She was certain I was having an affair but she'd convinced herself it was Clarice. When that turned out not to be so, she decided she'd been wrong about the whole thing and needed to make it up to me for being so suspicious. 'If you want to spend time with this Jonathan what's-his-name,' she said, 'by all means do.' Contrition is a great cover for us, looks like."

Brendan turned off the freeway onto Memorial Drive.

"You don't like that part of it, do you?" said Jonathan. "The deception."

"No. Not a bit. I have no experience with it. But I love the rest so much—being with you—that I . . . It seems so *right,* that's the problem." He stopped at a red light. "A month ago, this kind of thing had never occurred to me. Now it seems exactly right. And the other . . . my normal life . . . seems so empty."

He felt Jonathan's hand on his leg. He put his hand on top of Jonathan's and squeezed. The light changed, and he drove on, his right hand still holding Jonathan's.

"Complicated, isn't it?" he said.

"Yes," said Jonathan. "Maybe I was wrong about needing to hang on. Maybe I should . . ."

"You should do nothing but be yourself. And care about me as much as you can."

"That's an awful lot, you know. Getting to be more all the time."

Brendan squeezed Jonathan's hand again and put his own back on the steering wheel. He turned into the hospital parking garage. He found a place in a far, dark corner.

He reached over and touched Jonathan's cheek.

"I don't care how dangerous it is," he said. "I'm going to kiss you anyway."

Jonathan nodded. "I think you'd better."

They got out then and walked toward the elevator. On the main floor, as they neared the reception area, Brendan began to see people he knew.

"Hello, Doctor Garrison."

"Nice to see you, Doctor."

"Brendan! Working on the weekend? That's new. Give my love to Sandra."

The older woman at the reception desk was a good friend of his mother's, doing her volunteer work.

"Brendan, my dear," she said. "What a nice surprise. Visiting someone, or is this business?"

"A little of both. I'd like you to meet my friend, Jonathan Miles. Frances Markham."

They nodded.

"We sent a woman up from the Cumberland Clinic, and we've come to see how she is. Benson? Shantelle Benson?"

"I don't see that name here."

"She had a broken jaw, so she may still be in the OR."

"Let me call."

They waited.

"She is," said Frances. "Four West. Doctor Farnsworth is operating. Go on up."

They took the elevator to the fourth floor and turned right to the nurses' station.

"Doctor Garrison," said the nurse on duty. "I was wondering if you might . . . We heard you did the trake on this young woman we're working on now."

"I did, yes."

"Well, apparently you got to her in time. She's holding her own so far."

"Thank God for that. How much longer, do you think?"

She glanced at her computer screen.

"Half an hour, maybe. Forty-five minutes. They've replaced your trake tube and are finishing up setting the jaw."

"Jonathan here is from the Cumberland Clinic. Why don't we go get a cup of coffee and then check back with you a little later?"

"Good enough. I'll tell Doctor Farnsworth you're here."

They sat in the cafeteria, looking out the second-floor window, drinking their coffee. Neither spoke for a while.

"Interesting, isn't it?" said Jonathan.

"What is?"

"We don't have many pass-the-time things to say to each other."

"I find that very hopeful," said Brendan. "The world is full of casual chatter. What the world is not full of is the things we *do* have to say to each other."

Jonathan smiled. "Are you a philosopher?"

"More of one now than before I met you."

"Now, that *I* find very hopeful."

Brendan looked at his watch. "Twenty-five minutes. Shall we go up and see how they're doing?"

"Yes."

Back on the fourth floor, the nurse said, "Oh, here you are, Doctor Garrison. The patient's out of the OR, resting comfortably in ICU. She'll be under for a while yet, of course. But Doctor Farnsworth would like to see you. Let me tell him you're here."

A few minutes later, a large man with a red beard came through the door.

"Brendan, you sly dog." He held out his hand. Brendan shook it. "Trying to muscle in on my specialty here? Secret desire to be a surgeon after all?"

"Hardly. Matter of necessity, nothing more. This is my friend Jonathan Miles. Gregg Farnsworth." They shook hands. "Jonathan was working down at the clinic today when all this happened."

"Glad to meet you, Jonathan. So were you, Brendan, it appears. Good job, I have to say. A little crude, but effective. You moonlighting at this place these days?"

"No. Just visiting."

"Lucky thing for that woman. Still, my New Age friends insist there are no coincidences. Maybe they're right."

"Maybe. What's your prognosis?"

"Good, I'd say. We'll have to wait till she comes out of the anesthetic to be sure, but I'm guessing there'll be no ill effects from the lack of oxygen. We've wired up her jaw. Two breaks there—bad ones. And a fracture in her cheekbone. Looks like someone smacked her around pretty good. But she's young and apparently strong, so we'll see."

"Thanks, Gregg."

"Well, I'd better get going. People lined up waiting for my magic fingers to do their work. See you around, Brendan. Jonathan."

Outside the front door, Brendan looked at his watch.

"Damn," he said. "It's after five already. I'd better head on home. Shall I drop you off on the way?"

"No need," said Jonathan. "I can walk from here. Save you a little time."

The last thing Brendan wanted to do was save time. Leave Jonathan.

"This afternoon didn't turn out at all like I thought it was going to," he said. "I thought we'd have a chance to . . ."

"I did, too," said Jonathan. "But you know in a strange way, this was as . . ."

"Yes. It was. I couldn't possibly feel closer to you than I do at this moment."

"Nor I. You were splendid. You really were. But . . . you'd better get going."

"I had." Brendan hesitated. "I just wish . . ."

Jonathan nodded. "It's okay. It'll be okay."

They shook hands, and Jonathan turned and walked away. Brendan watched him for a minute, then headed for the parking garage.

Sandra was upstairs in their bedroom, sitting at her dressing table brushing her hair. Brendan burst into the room, eager for her to hear his news. He sat on the edge of the bed and told her about the clinic, about Shantelle, about his unexpected debut as a surgeon. Sandra stopped brushing and turned to stare at him.

"I've just come from Sloane," he said. "Looks like she's going to be all right. So far."

"Have you lost your mind?" said Sandra.

"What?"

"I can't believe this. Are you trying to bankrupt us? Ruin us completely?"

"What are you talking about?"

"Liability, my darling. Lawsuits. You've heard of them. I just . . ." She put her hand to her forehead. "I mean, think of it. If things *hadn't* gone well. If that woman had died while you were playing surgeon, slicing around on her throat, what do you think would've happened? Her family would've just said, graciously, 'Oh, well, he did his best'? I doubt it."

"How could I not have helped? I knew what needed to be done, and I had a responsibility to do it."

She shook her head.

"Your responsibility is to your family, never to put our future in this kind of jeopardy. I just can't believe you would do such a thing."

"If I'd done nothing, that young woman would've died. Or been as good as dead. Period. No question about it."

"But she was in a clinic, not a grocery store. Don't they have people there to handle emergencies?"

"Not today, they didn't. Just me."

"You were *visiting* there, Brendan. Just looking around. You were under no obligation to go riding to the rescue. You're not the doctor to the world, for pity's sake. Your own patients, fine—the ones your liability insurance is intended to cover. Not some woman off the streets."

Brendan stared at her. Was this the Sandra he'd known all these years? Not a fair question. He was certainly not the Brendan she thought she knew.

"Maybe in the old days," she said. "When everybody believed in the Hippocratic oath and all of that. Heroes may've been fine back then, but not now. This is the age of litigation, in case you hadn't noticed, and running around playing Good Samaritan is just too dangerous. I mean . . . you can't trust those people. If they see a chance to grab some of what we've got, they're sure to take it."

This was too much. His anger flared.

"Careful, Sandra," he said.

"Oh, I know. This new friend of yours is black, so of course you're more . . . and I'm sure he *is* different. Educated and charming, no doubt. But why he had to get you involved in this mess, I'll never know."

"Mess?"

His voice rose. *Hold your temper,* he thought.

"I saved a woman's life, Sandra."

"Yes, and risked ours. For heaven's sake, Brendan. Don't you see? Aren't you listening? We could've lost everything."

One more, he thought. *I'll give it one more try.*

"If I hadn't done what I did," he said, "*I'd* have lost everything."

"What on earth are you talking about?"

"How could I have lived with myself if I'd stood by and done nothing?"

"Easy. The same way you lived with yourself before. It's very simple. That woman *wasn't* your responsibility. You didn't hit her. You didn't break her jaw. You weren't employed by that clinic. They should've seen to it that someone qualified was around to take care of an emergency like that. It was *their* responsibility, not yours."

Brendan shook his head.

"Let's just drop this, okay?"

"Oh, no," she said. "I'm not going to drop it till you promise me you'll never do such a reckless thing, ever again."

He stared at her, his anger rising.

"Promise me!" she said.

"No, Sandra," he said. "No. I won't."

12

Sandra slipped into that cool, polite, but distant mood to which she retreated when her will was too forcefully challenged. Always before, Brendan had done whatever was necessary to bring her out of it—concern, flowers, attention, a gift. This time he left her there.

The next morning, they all performed their Sunday ritual. Up at eight, everyone sleeping a little later than on other days. Out the door by nine fifteen. Sunday school at quarter of ten. Church at eleven. Brendan and Sandra spoke to each other, at breakfast and on the way to town. Said the things they usually said when the family was going somewhere together. Chatter about who's ready, who's not, let's get going, nice day out, leave Joshua alone, Heather.

This time it was mostly a charade for the children's benefit. But they weren't fooled. Joshua wasn't, at any rate. In the Jeep's big rear-view mirror, Brendan could see his son's eyes. They were wary, shifting from Sandra to Brendan and back again.

Church was as it always was. Well-dressed, comfortable people being pious and sincere. Beautiful music. Calm, soothing words about love and duty.

They stopped for lunch at the steak house on East Rutherford. A cool, polite meal—the tension, Brendan realized, making the children uneasy enough to remain quiet through most of it, their eyes rarely leaving their plates. Should he say something? Try to make it easier for them? He should, but he didn't.

As soon as they got home, Brendan changed into jeans and a sweatshirt, went to his study, and finished the mystery he'd been reading. It was absorbing enough to keep his attention from wandering, and he was grateful for that.

When he put the book down, pleased that he'd figured everything out near the end, it was only ten after three. No way did he want to leave this room. Find out what the others were doing outside it. He sat for a minute, looking around—at the carved mahogany desk, the Turkish rug they'd bought in Istanbul and shipped home, the floor-to-ceiling bookshelves at the far end of the study, filled with the books he cared the most about. This was a place he loved and felt safe in.

He got up, walked over, reached up to the second shelf from the top, and took down the leather-bound edition of *Leaves of Grass* his father had given him for his eighteenth birthday. He had vague memories of having read it, long ago—and being strangely stirred by it. He flipped through the softly padded volume and began to read:

> Here to put your lips upon mine I permit you,
> With the comrade's long-dwelling kiss
>   or the new husband's kiss,
> For I am the new husband and I am the comrade.
> Or if you will, thrusting me beneath your clothing,
> Where I may feel the throbs of your heart
>   or rest upon your hip,
> Carry me when you go forth over land or sea;
> For thus merely touching you is enough, is best,
> And thus touching you would I silently sleep
>   and be carried eternally.

> Passing stranger! you do not know how longingly
>   I look upon you,
> You must be he I was seeking, . . .
> I am to think of you when I sit alone or wake
>   at night alone,
> I am to wait, I do not doubt I am to meet you again,
> I am to see to it that I do not lose you.

> O tan-faced prairie-boy,
> Before you came to camp came many a welcome gift,
> Praises and presents came and nourishing food,
>   till at last among the recruits,

You came, taciturn, with nothing to give—
   we but look'd on each other,
When lo! more than all the gifts of the world you gave me.

Brendan sat and stared at the wall. Did his father have any idea of
the depth of passion this book contained? How could he, and still give
it to his son, at that young and impressionable age? But people hadn't
known, had they? Or hadn't acknowledged it. This was great poetry,
by common consent. Odd and not entirely comprehensible, but great
nevertheless, and that's what mattered.

Besides, his father had run no risk, as it turned out. Brendan had
read it—but had eluded the call it surely made to that part of himself
he'd so carefully locked away.

   O tan-faced prairie-boy,

   I am to think of you when I sit alone or wake
      at night alone.

What Brendan wanted more than anything, just then, was to talk
with Jonathan, just for a minute, to see how he was, what he was doing. But he was hesitant to phone from the house and risk making
things even worse.

Monday morning, on his way to work, he did call from his car, as
soon as he was out of sight of his house. And Tuesday morning. And
Wednesday. The first two were mostly to keep in touch. A chance to
hear Jonathan's voice and feel close to him.

On Wednesday morning, Brendan asked, "What night does your
choir rehearse?"

"Thursday."

"Thank goodness. Any chance you might be home tonight?"

"For you?"

"Yes."

"Every chance. I was going out with friends—dinner and a movie—but I'll cancel it."

"You don't have to . . ."

"Of course I don't have to, but I will. What's up?"

"Sandra has to go out. Planning meeting for the big breast cancer gala. A ball the end of this month down at the Radisson. She says she'll be late."

"Well, then come on over. When can you get here?"

"Seven thirty, more or less."

"See you then."

Brendan's day at the office seemed to creep along, slow and tedious. Sniffles. Aches. Complaints. He couldn't wait for it to end. At dinner, Sandra was still polite, still distant. As soon as she had finished and gone off to her meeting, Brendan kissed the children, said good night to them, told Marva he was leaving, and went to be with Jonathan.

13 ♪♫♪

This time their lovemaking was less feverish for Brendan—warmer, more intimate, more fun. Afterward, Jonathan lay beside Brendan, his head on Brendan's shoulder, his arm across Brendan's chest. Brendan felt full, somehow. This was not just a man with a handsome face and a strong, muscular body that excited him. This was also a man with a large and generous heart. Brendan had the clear sense that he was holding not just that body but that heart as well, and all it contained. He felt this knowledge sinking deep inside him, down to places that hadn't been touched in years—if ever.

Jonathan stretched and sighed.

"Happy?" Brendan asked.

"Very."

"Even though we can't . . . ? I mean, even though it's so . . . unpredictable?"

"Well," said Jonathan. "That *is* a problem, I have to admit. Of course I wish it could be different, for both our sakes. But I wonder how much good that'll do—worrying about things we can't control. Maybe we should just be happy for what we've got."

Brendan kissed the side of Jonathan's head. Jonathan rubbed his hand gently up and down across the pale blond hairs on Brendan's chest.

"Tell me about you—a little," said Jonathan. "Your life. I don't know much about you, really."

"There's not much to tell."

"Don't be silly. There's a *lot*. There has to be."

"Well . . . how far back?"

"You were born here?"

"Oh, yes. Right here. At Sloane Memorial, in fact."

"You're an only child?"

"No. It just seems that way. My sister's a good bit older. Ten years. She lives out in Seattle. A high-tech whiz."

"Then you were one of those late-life surprises?"

"No, indeed. They were determined to have a son. It just took a while to accomplish it. Though I don't imagine anyone who knew them well was the least bit surprised when it happened. My parents don't like taking 'no' for an answer. Even from life."

"Are they really that formidable?"

"More. Much more. Take the most formidable people you've ever known, and double that. Triple it."

"Both of them?"

"Oh, my, yes. If anything, my mother's even more awe inspiring than my father. In fact, a good many people attribute much—maybe most—of his success in politics to her."

"Does he?"

"More than anyone else. Each is the other's biggest fan. So much so that . . ."

"What?"

"Nothing."

"No, you don't. If you're this hesitant about saying it, it's far from nothing. What?"

"It's just . . . they've always been so wrapped up in each other, and together in his career, that there wasn't much room left for me."

"Surely they love you . . ."

"Fiercely. Overwhelmingly. I'm the bright star in their firmament. No. I'm not talking about love. I'm talking about there not being much room for me in their lives."

Jonathan nodded.

"What did they do? Before?"

"Both lawyers. Garrison and Garrison. Quite a team. She was one of the first women in this part of the world to even go to law school, never mind actually settle down and practice. He did the corporate law. She did the trial work. Even more amazing—a woman in the courtroom back then. She just didn't let anyone get in her way. There are stories—family stories—about men who tried. Prosecutors. Judges. Town fathers. She either charmed them or ran right over them, whichever worked best."

"When did your father go into politics?"

"Soon after they were married. Which was . . . when? Nineteen fifty-three. He'd been thinking about it, even back in law school where they met. She gave him the push he needed."

"To run for what?"

"School board first. Start small and work up. That's how they did it in those days. He won, and before long he was head of that. Then city council. Before long he was chairman of that. Then the state legislature."

"Then Washington."

"Yeah. Nineteen seventy-four. Nixon had resigned, and the Republican Party here was looking for a fresh, untainted face. My father was it."

"I do my best to avoid thinking about that."

"What?"

"That your family is full of Republicans."

Brendan laughed and kissed the side of Jonathan's head.

"Try not to let it bother you."

"I do. But my mother? Never! My guess is she'd be far more upset about *that* than about your being white."

"You mean . . . it would upset her? My being white?" Brendan was genuinely surprised.

"Yes, indeed. She grew up in the *very* segregated South. Cheered for Rosa Parks and Martin Luther King. Made an exception for Kennedy. She loved him. Hated Nixon and George Wallace. Thought Reagan was a fool. You get the idea."

"And you?"

"Loved Clinton. Absolutely loved him. Hated Jesse Helms and Newt Gingrich. Still hate Tom DeLay. Thought Reagan was a fool."

Brendan laughed again.

"I guess we won't be discussing politics much," he said. "If we're wise."

"I guess not. So your father went to Congress in nineteen seventy-four. You must have been very young."

"Just starting fourth grade. Oh—I hadn't realized. About the age Joshua is now."

"Did you go to Washington with them?"

"No. They wanted me to finish grade school here at least, give me a feeling of having roots in this place, so they parked me with my uncle, my father's older brother. Dorothy, my sister, was in college already, which meant I was pretty much alone."

"Cousins? At your uncle's, where you lived?"

"Also older. Two boys in college. A girl still at home. Senior in high school. Her interests did not include me."

"Sounds rough."

"I didn't think of it that way at the time. My parents came home some weekends, and whenever Congress was in recess, and all summer, of course. We lived at home, together, while they were here."

"Did you like your uncle?"

"He was great. Jovial. Lots of fun, unlike my father. He owned the Coca-Cola bottling plant here in town, and I used to love to go down and watch all that marvelous machinery in motion. He died last year."

"I'm sorry." Jonathan was quiet for a minute. "What about high school?"

"St. Albans in Washington. Prep school for the elite. I was there when my father first ran for the Senate—and won, of course. Very exciting time. I worked on his campaign. Traveled around the state with them all summer, and took some time off from school that fall. I even made a few speeches along the way."

"I wish I could've heard you."

"I was pretty good, as a matter of fact."

"I can imagine. Is that something you thought about doing? Going into politics?"

"It's what I was supposed to do. What my parents had in mind. Groomed me for. The heir apparent, which I guess is why I didn't do it."

"Your own rebellion?"

"They saw it that way."

"Must've been difficult."

"It was. But I just held on. Besides, I picked a very acceptable alternative. My son, the doctor. You know."

"Did you choose it because you loved medicine?"

"Mmm. Did I? Yes, I think so. I *hope* so. Making people well. I loved the idea of that."

"You didn't love the idea of politics?"

"Much more complicated, I'm afraid. I didn't want to *do* it, as a matter of right. Just slide into it like that, without having to earn it. Even so, I found politics very seductive. Still do.

"I grew up knowing powerful people. Especially those years in Washington. The Reagan years, with apologies to you and your mother. Our apartment was always full of movers and shakers. I even went to a state dinner at the White House. I *loved* the pomp and grandeur, I can tell you. The sheer snobbery of it. All that power."

"All that money."

"Not so impressive to me, because I've always had it. More than enough at first, then . . . too much from then on."

"Too much." Jonathan shook his head. "Imagine. You've got too much. I've got enough. So many others have way too little."

"Is this one of those political discussions we're not going to have?"

"Probably. But it'll be back, what do you want to bet?"

Brendan smiled. "I bet it will."

"It's all fascinating, but . . . know what I'd rather be doing right now?"

"What's that?"

"This."

Jonathan pulled Brendan over on top of him.

When Brendan got home, a little before ten thirty, Sandra wasn't there. She *was* late. Fine with him.

He found a note from Marva on the bulletin board in the kitchen. His mother had called. She and the senator would be flying in from Washington Friday afternoon. Dinner at their house that evening at eight. As always, it was more of a summons than an invitation. Adults only, please. They'd see the children over the weekend.

Brendan checked the calendar Sandra kept next to the bulletin board. No conflicts. He wrote the information in the square for Friday and left the note on the bulletin board for Sandra to see.

He drank a glass of water and went upstairs to bed.

14

On Thursday afternoon, Brendan sat at his desk, writing on Evan McIver's chart. Type 2 diabetes. Undiagnosed for too long. Sores beginning to develop on the left foot.

His buzzer rang.

"Yes?" he said.

"Ms. Nichols on line four. Are you available?"

"Yes. Thank you, Cathy."

He punched the button and picked up the receiver.

"Clarice?"

"I won't keep you long, Brendan. I know you must be busy. I've been wanting to be in touch, but . . . I don't know. So much easier to just put it off."

"I don't blame you."

"It was truly one of the most bizarre experiences of my life. That phone call."

"I'll bet."

"Are you all right? You and Sandra?"

"Yes. We're fine."

Pretty smooth for someone not used to lying, he thought.

"I'm glad," she said. "I mean . . . it's so ridiculous!"

"Oh?"

"Well, sure. Just look at you. Mr. Rectitude. Most anybody else, no surprise at all. But *you?* I mean, I wouldn't have thought you'd have the time, for heaven's sake. Or the imagination."

Brendan laughed.

"I wouldn't have thought so, either."

"Well, I just wanted to be in touch. We can still be friends, can't we?"

"Forever," said Brendan. "As far as I'm concerned."

Toward the end of the afternoon, Brendan's buzzer rang again.

"Can you take a call from that Mr. Miles?"

"Yes, certainly."

"Line two."

"Jonathan?"

"Sorry to disturb you like this."

"You're not. Not you."

"Thanks. I've just been to the hospital. To check up on Shantelle."

"Good for you. How is she?"

"Much better. Improving every day. The thing is, they're keeping her there a while longer. Bringing in a physical therapist, to help her learn to talk and eat again."

"That's wonderful news."

"Wonderful, yes. But puzzling, don't you think? They should be tossing her out by now, an indigent patient like her. I've been around long enough to know how they operate. *Have* to operate, to be fair. So somebody's got to be paying for them to keep her in this long."

"You think so?"

"Don't be coy with me, Brendan. It has to be you. Is it?"

He didn't want anyone to know, outside the hospital, but Jonathan wasn't "anyone." He could lie to other people, for what he hoped were good reasons. But he couldn't lie to Jonathan.

"Yes," he said. "It's me."

"I thought so. It's terrific of you, of course. It really is. I don't know how she would have . . . but I feel bad about it, since I'm the one who got you involved. It's going to cost you a fortune. It'll have to. I do some of the bookkeeping for the clinic, so I know. I'd help out if I could, but I . . ."

"No, you won't. Don't worry about it. Please."

"But I do."

"Don't. I've got too much, remember? It's time I started spreading it around."

15

Brendan got home from the office a little before seven on Friday. Just enough time to see the kids for a minute and then head off for dinner with his parents. Sandra was in their bedroom, standing in front of the full-length mirror on her closet door, putting on a pair of earrings. She greeted him more warmly than she had all week and asked about his day. He said it had been fine. Busy, but fine.

She was wearing a lavender cashmere sweater and a long black skirt. Brendan would keep on the suit and tie he'd worn to the office. Dinners with his parents were not casual affairs.

When Sandra turned to face him, Brendan saw that she was wearing the string of pearls his father had given her on their wedding day. *She knows all about butter,* he thought, *and which side of the bread it goes on.*

In the car on the way to his parents' house, Sandra said, "Look. I'm sorry, honey. This has gone on long enough. Too long. So let's not be mad anymore, okay? I . . . I don't know what's getting into me lately. I'm just so edgy and out of sorts for some reason, and I'm taking it all out on you. I'm sorry. I know you wouldn't do anything to hurt me and the kids. Not intentionally."

No, he thought. *Please. Don't apologize. Not again. I should be the one.*

He turned in through the gate, waved to the security guard, and drove up the broad circular driveway toward the house in which he grew up. He was surprised to see three cars already in the parking area off to the left. *I wonder who?* he thought. He got out and walked around to where Sandra was waiting. She squeezed his arm and kissed his cheek.

"Better?" she asked.

"Yes," he said.

One of the maids opened the front door. Black dress, white apron, little white cap, black face.

"Evenin', Miz Garrison. Doctor."

"Hello, Josie," said Sandra.

Brendan smiled at her.

"How's your son?" he asked.

"Pretty well. Thanks for askin'. They're all in the front room. Take your coat, Miz Garrison?"

"Thank you, Josie."

Brendan and Sandra walked across the foyer into the large formal living room. His mother was near the fireplace, where a small fire crackled comfortably. His father was over by the sideboard pouring what was undoubtedly scotch into a glass. He could see District Attorney Peters and his wife, Judge Maddox and her husband. Jock Rawlings, the local congressman, and his brand-new, very young wife. And a couple he didn't know. *Full house,* he thought.

His mother excused herself from Arlene Maddox and came toward them, regal in dark green. She kissed Sandra first.

"How nice you look," she said.

"Thank you, Pauline," said Sandra.

Then she kissed Brendan.

"And you, my dear. Everything all right with you?"

"Yes. Things are going very well."

Smooth as glass. He was getting good at this.

"We apologize for being out of touch for so long, your father and I. We got your e-mails and saw your number on the caller ID. But we've been particularly busy these past few months. Election year, you know. Stanley gets so wrapped up in it—every time. Even years like this when he's not running himself. In fact, we've brought a national committeeman home with us, Grant Beresford. He and Stanley have 'things to discuss.' His wife is someone you ought to get along with, Sandra. Let me introduce you both."

Brendan spoke to those he passed as he crossed the room behind his mother and Sandra.

"Grant and Deirdre Beresford. My daughter-in-law Sandra. My son Brendan."

Murmurs of pleasure all around. Pauline moved the two women toward the fireplace, leaving Brendan alone with Grant. His father came directly over.

"Wonderful to see you, son. You're looking well."

"So are you. You never age a day from one visit to the next."

His father laughed his hearty, booming laugh, the one that had endeared him to generations of voters.

"I don't, do I? It's doing what you love that keeps you young. And I do love politics. The horse race. Who's ahead, who's behind, and why. Fighting the good fight—and making sure you win."

"Then having a chance to do so much good," said Brendan. "After you *have* won."

The senator laughed again.

"Well, yes, of course," he said. "That's why we do it." He turned to Grant. "You see what I mean? Quite a boy I've got here."

"Yes, indeed," said Grant. "You're a doctor, I understand."

"Internist. Family medicine. It's what I love best."

"Very admirable. Though it's a hard time for doctors, as we all know. For everyone connected with health care. People so upset with the HMOs and the insurance companies—the very groups that have done the most to keep costs from rising even faster."

"It's a complicated subject, of course," said Brendan. "The question of who has control over final decisions and who gets what kind of treatment."

"Complicated?" said the senator. "You don't know the half of it. I've just come from a series of hearings on the Hill. More of our attempts to bring a little sanity to the whole Medicare fiasco. Privatize as much as we can, and give the free market a chance to work its magic. But do you think those benighted Democrats will even try to listen to reason? Oh, no. They're so busy pampering and accomodating, they've got no time for . . ."

Brendan could feel himself retreating, closing up. *The way I always do when I'm with my father,* he thought. *I'm the doctor. He's the expert on medical care.* Brendan listened to the conversation, mostly a monologue by his father. He nodded. Grant nodded. The senator lectured.

Brendan felt a hand on his arm and turned. Arlene Maddox was smiling at him.

"Hello, Judge," he said. "It's been a while."

"Too long. How are the children?"

"Growing so fast I'm afraid to leave the house in the morning, for fear they'll be off to college by the time I get home."

She laughed.

"I know what you mean. Mine *are* in college now. Both of them."

"They can't be."

"Yes, they are. No drink?"

"I haven't gotten that far yet."

"Let's head on over, then. I'm ready for a refill."

Brendan nodded to Grant, who smiled and nodded at him. The senator glanced at Brendan, nodded, and turned back to Grant without missing a beat.

". . . absolute necessity of keeping costs under control. I hate to think how much more expensive it's going to be if we don't find a way to get a handle on all these lawsuits that are . . ."

Brendan made Arlene a manhattan and poured himself a glass of wine. He chatted with her for a while—about her children, his children—then started making the rounds of the other guests.

He had always been fond of Andy Peters, a gruff, no-nonsense former prosecutor who'd been district attorney for maybe five years. Their conversation was mostly about the recent increase in drug use among teenagers in the area. Very disturbing, said Andy. Those housing projects down on the South Side were the worst by far.

"I just don't understand it. The faster we lock 'em up, the more keep popping up to take their place."

Shouldn't this be telling you something? thought Brendan. But he didn't say that. He came at it from a more tactful angle.

"What about treatment?" he asked. "Wouldn't that be more effective? And quite a lot cheaper besides."

Andy shook his head.

"Doesn't work. Hard for you laymen to understand, of course, but coddling those people just doesn't work. Take it from me. Firmness— consistent firmness—is all they understand. No. What we have to do is keep the pressure on—hard. Keep building prisons to hold 'em. As many as it takes. Then, once we've gotten the deadbeats off the streets and safely inside, the rest of us'll be free to get on with our lives. Without having to worry about all these disruptions."

Brendan had known Jock Rawlings—overweight, blustery, a little raucous—all his life. Brendan usually found him tedious, and tonight was no exception. He talked loudly, unendingly, about his reelection. He was a shoo-in, naturally—just as he'd been the five times before this—but he was taking no chances. He told Brendan all about how much money he'd raised, and from whom—agribusiness, utility companies, financial institutions—and about the television ads he had planned for the summer and fall, which he was sure would wipe out any faint hope his opponent might have had.

This opponent, a young consumer advocacy lawyer named Julia Fletcher, was out of step with their district, he said, on two important issues. His ads would portray her pro-choice views as the moral equivalent of murder, and her anti-death penalty views as soft on crime. The irony of Jock's own opposing views—for life at the beginning, for death later on—was not lost on Brendan, but seemed to escape Jock entirely.

Brendan would have loved to simply walk away—or better yet, to work up the courage to tell Jock how tiresome he was, and how pompous he sounded when he talked like this. But there was no way Brendan would ever say such things to him, certainly not in his father's house. So he stayed and listened. In the middle of one of Jock's long-winded spiels, however, Grant Beresford and the senator called to Jock from across the room. He excused himself and hurried over— and Brendan was rescued.

He turned to Jock's new wife, Marilyn, who'd been standing, silent and attentive, beside her husband through all of this. Brendan soon discovered that she was not at all what he had expected. Gossips all over town, his wife included, had portrayed her as a young, pretty gold digger dazzled by Jock's power and prestige. She *was* young and pretty, that much was true. But, Brendan found, she was also intelligent, articulate, and full of confidence in her own abilities. She had a master's degree in government from Yale and was working on her doctorate in international relations at Georgetown University. Brendan liked her right away and found her slant on politics—slightly cynical, from close personal observation, yet still hopeful—fascinating. But even though Sandra was engrossed with Deirdre Beresford over on the sofa, he was careful not to talk to Marilyn too long.

Dinner was delicious, as always. Crabmeat bisque. Rack of lamb, with wild rice and fresh peas. Salad. Crème brûlée. Served by *two* maids—Josie and her sister Tina. They came in each time Pauline rang her little crystal bell. Plates down. Food. Plates up. New plates down. More food. Wine through it all. White with the soup. Red with the lamb.

Arlene Maddox, sitting on Brendan's left, was well beyond tipsy. The senator's face was taking on the redness of too many scotches, followed by all this wine. Loud laughter around the table made it clear that many of the others were also feeling no pain. Isabel Peters, however, on Brendan's right, was drinking sparkling water and was therefore quite sober. He enjoyed her stories about her trip to Nepal. She'd gone with a group that trekked high into the mountains to spend time at a Buddhist monastery. The peace and serenity, she said, were beyond anything she'd ever experienced. She'd been home for eight months but was still finding it hard to adjust.

Back into the living room for coffee and liqueurs. People sat around chatting, laughing. Josie and Brendan's mother helped his wobbly father up to bed. Jock and Marilyn Rawlings were the first to leave, with the Maddoxes not far behind.

At the door, his mother kissed Sandra, then him. Sandra walked toward the car.

"We'll be flying out early on Tuesday," said Pauline, "and we're booked solid until then, I'm afraid. But the next trip, we'll be sure to set aside more time for you."

"That would be nice," said Brendan. "I'll look forward to it."

"So lovely to see you, my dear," she said. "It always is. You are my treasure. You know that."

"I do."

"Keep in touch, now."

"I will, Mother. Give my love to Father. Safe trip."

She waved and went back into the house.

Sandra, who'd apparently been too busy talking to drink much, chattered about her new friend all the way home.

"Deirdre has her own interior design firm. Isn't that exciting? Does homes for congressmen's wives. And senators, of course. Though they don't turn over nearly as often. Sort of an old-girls' network. One introduces her to the next. She does very well. So charming. No wonder.

"I've invited her over for tea on Sunday afternoon. That'll give me time to round up some of the women she'd be most likely to enjoy. Lara and Ingrid, for sure, and maybe Trish. Although I don't know. She can be so boring. She'll want to go on and on about what she's done to her house. No. Maybe not Trish. But Adele. And Barbie! She'll love Barbie.

"Oh, but that means I won't be able to pick the kids up after they've had lunch with Pauline and Stanley. Pauline wants to take them home from church and then have one of us pick them up around three or so. Looks like that'll be you. You don't mind, do you?"

"Not at all."

16 🎵

The next morning after breakfast, Sandra turned from the sink and said, "Let's split the kids today, Brendan. You keep Joshua occupied, and I'll take Heather with me."

"All right," said Brendan.

"I need to go by the florist's. Talk with the caterer. Buy a new dress. Oh, and stop by Ingrid's for a while. It'll take hours. Heather will love all that, but Joshua would be bored stiff. So you keep an eye on him, okay?"

"Sure. Is there anything he needs to do today? Someplace I ought to take him?"

"No," she said. "Lucky you. You can do whatever you like, the two of you."

"Good." He nodded. "We'll think of something."

"Marva's gone to see about her mother—poor thing, that hip's still not healing right—so get some lunch for yourselves. Out preferably. I don't think there's much here you could manage."

He didn't respond to that.

"Well," she said, rummaging in her purse, "I guess that's it." She took her keys out and snapped the purse shut. "You all set?"

"Yes."

"See you late afternoon, then."

"Fine."

She waved from the kitchen door and was gone. He sipped his coffee and looked out across the backyard toward the pool. Time to think about getting it cleaned up and ready to fill.

Heather came running in, her arms outstretched. He hugged her close to him.

"Bye, Daddy," she said.

He kissed the top of her head.

"Bye, sweetheart. You have fun with Mommy."

"I will."

She pulled him down toward her, kissed his cheek, and ran out of the room. The sweet smell of her bath powder lingered in the air. He heard car doors slamming and the Jeep pulling out of the driveway. He took his cup and saucer to the sink, rinsed them, and put them in the dishwasher.

He walked up the stairs and down the hall to Joshua's room. He stopped in the doorway. Joshua was sitting at his desk by the window, his head bent over a pad of paper. A tightness pulled at Brendan's throat and chest. His son. Bright. Studious. Quieter, more self-contained, than the friends who came to visit him. Brendan would happily have stood there a while, just watching, but Joshua looked up, brushed his hair back, and smiled.

"Hi, Dad," he said.

"Hi." Brendan looked at Joshua's face. It was lengthening, becoming more defined. Its baby cheeks, the chubbiness that had made him so adorable, were long gone. Was he nine yet? Not quite. Not till August.

"Something wrong, Dad?" asked Joshua.

Brendan smiled.

"No," he said. "Not at all. I was just thinking that boring parent thing—how fast you're growing up."

"Doesn't seem very fast to me."

"No," said Brendan. "I guess it doesn't. Heather and your mom are off running errands, and Marva's got things to do today, so it's just us. You and me. What shall we do?"

Joshua shrugged. "Whatever you say."

Brendan frowned. "What would *you* like to do?"

"I don't care."

"C'mon, son. Help me out here. What were you planning to do?"

"Stay here and work on this, I guess."

"What is it?"

"Homework."

"Oh? What kind?"

"Arithmetic. Has to be done by Monday."

"Should I just leave you alone and let you keep working on it, then?"

Joshua shrugged again. "No. Not if . . . you were thinking we might go someplace?"

"Yes. Any ideas?"

"Well . . . I . . . maybe it's too much."

"What?"

"I've been wishing I could get out to the lake sometime. To the state park over there. Because . . ."

"Go on."

"Well, we're studying trees in Cub Scouts now, and I . . . Do you think we could take my book out there? See if I can learn how to identify some of them? Would that be all right? Our scoutmaster said it would be a good place to go."

"Absolutely. That's a great idea."

"It's not too far?"

"We've got all day. Don't need to be back till dinnertime."

"You don't have things you wanted to do yourself?"

"Nope. Not today. Just be with you. I'll go change into some jeans and hunt up my hiking boots. Meet you downstairs?"

Joshua smiled, a big smile.

"You bet!" he said.

On the way out of town, Joshua talked about school, the science fair coming up, a field trip his class would be taking to the new Children's Museum.

"Sounds like you're very busy," said Brendan.

"I am," said Joshua.

He talked a while about the Pokémon cards he was organizing, then about his soccer team. How much better he was playing this year. Once he got off on subjects he was comfortable with, Joshua was fine. Brendan was relieved and happy to listen.

They turned off the interstate onto a smaller road. Before long, the lake, wide at this end, came into view. They drove down a hill through some woods and stopped at a T intersection. The lake spread out in front of them.

"Which way?" asked Brendan.

Joshua looked at the signs across the road.

"This way," he said, pointing right.

Small houses stood side by side, facing toward the water. A few boats bobbed at their moorings. As the road went back into the woods, Brendan saw a sign that said Lake Carson State Park. Just past it was a picnic area, off to the right.

"Shall we park here?" he asked.

"I guess so," said Joshua. "Lots of trees, that's for sure."

Brendan drove to the far end of the lot and parked. They got out. Joshua slung his backpack over his shoulder and walked toward the woods. Brendan locked the car.

"Dad? This sign over here says Nature Trail. Could we go on it?"

"Sure. You lead the way."

They walked a few minutes in silence. The breeze, just cool enough to be refreshing, felt good.

"Look, Dad!" said Joshua. "Some of the trees've got name tags on them. Awesome! This one's called . . . wait . . . *sigh*-ca-more?"

He looked up at Brendan, puzzled.

"*Sick*-a-more," said Brendan.

"Oh. Right."

Joshua took a book out of his backpack, checked the index, and turned to a page near the middle. He read from the book: "'Has an enlarged base, straight trunk, and spreading branches.'" He looked up at the tree and back at the book. "'The sycamore grows to a larger trunk diameter than any other native hardwood. Leaves turn brown in the fall. Grows in wet soils of stream banks and at the edge of lakes.'" He looked around. "Sure does," he said. "Is it all right to take a leaf, do you think?"

Brendan looked for a sign that might tell them, but there wasn't one. Just the names on the trees.

"I think it's all right, since it's for your project. But only one of each kind."

"That's what I think, too. Could you reach me a leaf from that branch, please? From the sycamore?"

Brendan did.

Joshua sat on the ground, traced an outline of the leaf in his notebook, labeled it, and pressed the leaf between the pages.

Another tree. Another leaf. Another pressing. Beech. Cottonwood. Black willow. Hickory. By now, mid-April, most of the leaves seemed to be out. A few were still a bright early green.

Brendan carried either the identification book or the notebook, whichever one Joshua wasn't using. The woods smelled damp, mossy. Birds called every now and then. Squirrels chattered. Brendan had never been in these woods in his life, but he felt peaceful here, connected to them in a way that puzzled him.

Joshua was reading aloud again: "'The Northern Red Oak is a large tree with a rounded crown. Its bark is dark gray and rough, furrowed into ridges . . .'"

They walked along the trail, which looped away from the lake and back around to the picnic area. It was almost one o'clock when they got to the car.

"Hungry?" asked Brendan.

"You bet!"

"Let's see what we can find."

They drove around the lake and came to a town, small but somehow charming. On the left were a gas station and a general store with a big sign in the window that said BAIT. On the right were a café and laundromat.

The café was a rustic place. Formica-covered tables and an odd mixture of chairs. Joshua ordered a hamburger, Brendan a bowl of vegetable soup and a salad. Joshua took out his notebook and studied the leaves, one at a time.

Brendan looked around. An older couple—in their sixties, maybe early seventies—sat at a table across the room. He talked. She looked at her plate as she ate. A bulletin board on the wall to Brendan's left advertised things for rent: camping sites, boats, canoes, cabins.

A group of five young people—three men, two women—came in, loud and boisterous. Their boots clumped as they went to a large table near the back. Their noisy conversation filled the room.

On the way out, Brendan asked, "How was your hamburger?"

"Great," said Joshua. "I liked it."

"Have you got enough leaves, do you think?"

"For now, anyway. I need to learn the ones I've got before I look for any more."

"Shall we drive the rest of the way around the lake, then, before we head for home?"

"Whatever you say."

17

As was true so often recently, Brendan couldn't sleep. His mind was too full. He'd enjoyed his day with Joshua, quite a lot, but it had also disturbed him. He knew so little about his son. He knew what his interests were. Some of them. But he didn't know *him*.

He turned on his side. Didn't like that position any better. Lay again on his back. Sandra was breathing steadily, the sound he recognized as deep, untroubled sleep. Even this tea tomorrow, which had obsessed her all day and evening, wasn't enough to disturb her slumber. Did he admire that, the way she could put things into compartments? He wasn't sure.

The clock on his bedside table said two seventeen. He got up, pulled on a sweatshirt and a pair of sweatpants, tiptoed out of the room, and went downstairs through the kitchen onto the back porch. He sat in one of the big wicker rockers.

It was a beautiful spring night, chilly and clear. A three-quarter moon cast shadows across the yard. He could hear peepers off in the distance and an occasional dog.

He thought, for some reason—the peepers maybe—of his own childhood. The years before his parents went to Washington. Even then, when all three of them still lived together, what was most clear in his mind was the loneliness. Sitting in rooms full of adults, listening respectfully, saying nothing. He must have said something, sometimes. He can't remember that he ever did. In his memory, he can hear his father talking, his mother talking, other people talking. But he can't hear the sound of his own voice.

Then his parents went away, and for a few years he lived most of the time with his uncle. No one anywhere near his age in the house. More loneliness. He doesn't remember feeling abandoned, just alone. He had friends in school, of course. But not close ones. Their fault or his? Hard to say. Did he hold himself aloof from them, or were they in awe of his father's position? Of his big house on the hill, behind a tall wrought-iron fence with ornate wrought-iron gates?

Most likely, the fault was his. He had a fence around himself as well, he thought, then and now. People couldn't get through it either. Not unless he opened the gate, and he didn't do that very often. Sandra was inside. Joshua and Heather. His parents. His sister, sort of. Clarice. And Jonathan. Jonathan most of all. Farthest inside. Closest to him. Closer, maybe, than anyone had ever been. How could that be? So quickly? And why? He had no idea.

What about Joshua? Was his childhood as lonely, as closed off? Brendan had no idea about that either.

He heard a car out on the street. It went on by. Someone coming home from a very late party, no doubt. The air felt good. Not a breeze exactly, just cool air moving ever so slightly as he rocked. A dog barked again.

What *about* Joshua? He seemed to have more friends than Brendan did at that age. How close were they? Brendan couldn't even make a guess. He wondered if Sandra knew. Probably not. The one who would know was Marva.

Brendan stared across the yard.

Was there anything he could do to make things easier for Joshua? He would try. From now on, he would do his best. He owed him that.

Heather? Brendan smiled. She was like her mother. She'd be fine. She knew what she wanted—already, at six and a half—and did what it took to get it. She'd be fine. But he ought to pay more attention to Joshua.

18

Even though he felt tired—and a little grumpy—Brendan was up by eight the next morning. He showered and shaved, ate breakfast with Sandra and the kids, and off they all went to Sunday school and church. The four of them sat with Brendan's parents during the service. Everyone in the place, it seemed, pressed toward them afterward to greet the senator and his wife. It took quite a while to work their way through the crowd waiting in the vestibule and on the sidewalk outside. Joshua and Heather were patient through it all, Brendan was pleased to see, and then rode off with their grandparents in the backseat of the chauffeured limousine.

Marva served Brendan and Sandra their lunch at the little table in the breakfast room. Sandra talked more than she ate, mostly to Marva—last-minute details about the tea. Which china to use. Which tablecloths. How to arrange the sandwiches and pastries. Where to put the flowers.

"Is Purlie here yet?" asked Sandra.

"Out in the laundry room, ironing napkins."

"Good."

She turned to Brendan.

"Don't forget, you have to pick the kids up around three."

"I remember," he said. "Anything else I can do to help?"

"I don't think so. But thanks for asking. We've got it under control, Marva and I. We're a good team."

"Indeed you are." He smiled. "I guess . . . maybe I'll go ahead and leave now, before all those cars start filling up the driveway."

"Good idea," she said. "Take a drive somewhere. Relax. It's a beautiful day."

"It is."

He stood up.

"I hope it all goes very well," he said. "Say hello to Deirdre for me."

"I will. See you later, then." She waved and turned back to Marva. "Now, if you'll finish polishing the silver, I'll put these dishes in the dishwasher and go look for that platter."

As Brendan drove toward town, he found himself wishing he could see Jonathan. At least talk to him. But he was tied up at his church. A luncheon and then some kind of meeting.

Brendan headed for Sloane Memorial. He stopped by the nurses' station on the fifth floor.

"Hello, Harriet. Nice to see you again."

"You, too, Doctor Garrison."

"Have you been taking care of Shantelle?"

"I have, off and on. Mostly on. And what a pleasure it's been. She's an amazing young woman."

"Is she? I haven't had a chance yet to find out."

"Well, she is. We're going to miss her."

"Oh?"

"Yes. She'll be leaving us on Tuesday. Her physical therapist says she's ready."

"Looks like I got here just in time."

"Yes, you did. Let me take you in. She'll be delighted to see you."

The room was halfway down the hall. Only one bed, over by the windows.

"Shantelle?" said the nurse. The young woman looked up from her book. "This is Doctor Garrison. He's the man who did the first tracheostomy, down at the clinic."

Shantelle's eyes filled with tears. She put out her hand. Brendan took it and held it. The nurse went back outside.

"How can I ever thank you enough?" said Shantelle. Her voice was soft, raspy. "You saved my life."

"Well . . . I helped, certainly."

She tried to smile, but the left side of her face was still swollen, and she was only partly successful. A light green scarf covered her throat.

"I know what you did," she said. "Please let me be grateful."

Brendan nodded.

"All right," he said.

He squeezed her hand and let it go. He pulled a chair over and sat next to the bed.

"Is it hard for you to talk?" he asked. "Still painful?"

"A little. But I'm supposed to try, for short periods of time. I can't think of a nicer way to do my practicing."

It was Brendan's turn to smile.

"Nor can I. What are you reading?"

"Toni Morrison. *The Bluest Eye*. Have you read it?"

"No. I haven't. *Beloved* and *Song of Solomon*, but not that one."

"You might want to give it a try."

"Thank you. I will. How's your mother?"

Again that attempt to smile.

"You want to talk about *grateful!* She thinks you walk on water. She'll be here later on this afternoon, and she . . ."

Shantelle swallowed. A look of pain crossed her face.

"Are you all right?" asked Brendan.

"Not exactly, but let me keep trying. Just a while longer."

"Of course."

"Mama will be so upset she missed you, although I guess it's for the best. She'd likely give you a two-hour lecture on how wonderful you are. How courageous."

Brendan smiled again.

"I could handle that," he said.

"You know, maybe you can help me."

"I'll try."

"It's just . . . I can't figure out how all this is being paid for. Private room. Such a long stay. So much therapy. You know, of course, that I don't have any kind of insurance, so I . . ."

"It's okay. Believe me. You don't have to worry about it."

"But I *do* worry. If they're expecting me to take care of even a small part of it, I'm afraid . . . I mean, much as I'd like to, there's no way I could . . ."

"Please. Put it out of your mind and just concentrate on getting well. I assure you it's all been taken care of."

"By the clinic?"

He hesitated. "In a way."

"Well, bless them for that. I don't see how I could have made it otherwise."

"Look," said Brendan. "I don't want to appear to be meddling in your life, but I can't help being concerned."

"About what?"

Her voice was hoarse, fading.

"The man who did this."

She turned away and looked out the window.

"You don't have to go back to that man. I've . . . did you live with him? Or he with you?"

"He lives with us. Mama and me."

"Then you have no place else to go?"

She looked directly at him.

"Why would I need someplace else?"

"For your own protection. I've taken the liberty of contacting a shelter, for women who've been . . . who can't go home."

"But that's not me, Doctor. I *can* go home. He won't hit me again."

"He might."

"He won't."

"Just till you're better. Your jaw is wired together and will take months to heal properly. You don't want to take a chance on anything happening till then. So—just for a couple of months?"

"You don't understand. I love him. And he loves me."

"That may well be, but . . . I don't mean to interfere. I honestly don't. But I feel so . . . responsible."

"It's all right. I appreciate that."

"Well, then . . ." He reached into his pocket and took out a piece of paper. He put it on the bed beside her. "Here are the address and phone number. Please. At least think about what I'm saying. Think about which you love more—him or your life. You only have one. Like all of us. You could've lost it. You know that. But you didn't. You've been given something not many people get—another chance. Don't throw it away. Grab hold of it. Make it count. Please."

Her eyes filled with tears again.

"Thank you, Doctor," she said, "for your concern. I *will* think about it. I promise."

19 🎵

A new security guard was on duty at Brendan's parents' house. Instead of opening the gate, he held up his hand. Brendan stopped, and the young man came to his window.

"Are you expected?" he asked.

"I'm Brendan Garrison, the senator's son. Yes, I'm expected."

"May I see some ID?"

Brendan's anger flared. Of all the nerve! He was tempted to say something sarcastic, but thought better of it. The man was new, after all. He reached into his jacket pocket for his wallet.

The guard nodded.

"Thank you, Mr. Garrison," he said. "Sorry for the inconvenience. You can't be too careful these days."

"No," said Brendan. "I guess you can't."

The guard pressed a button, and the gate swung open. Brendan drove toward the house. Josie let him in.

"They're out in the den, Doctor," she said.

Brendan stopped in the doorway. His father and mother were sitting in wingback chairs facing a small sofa, on which Joshua and Heather sat, upright, attentive, listening dutifully to their grandfather, who was talking loudly.

". . . have to understand how important your studies are. If you're ever going to make something of yourselves, you absolutely must . . ."

Brendan watched his son's face and felt suddenly very sad.

Pauline looked over. "Brendan, my dear. At last. We've been waiting for you."

"Daddy!" yelled Heather.

She jumped off the sofa and ran toward him. He leaned down to kiss her cheek. As he straightened, he glanced at his watch.

"It's only ten of three," he said.

His parents and Joshua were all standing now.

"Yes," said his mother. "But we have to be out at the club by three thirty."

"I see. Well, we'll head on home, then."

"If you don't mind," said the senator. "So many people to see, and so little time."

Brendan smiled. "I understand."

"We wouldn't have missed our visit with these beautiful children, though."

"No, of course not."

"They were perfect angels," said Pauline. "As usual."

"I'm sure they were," said Brendan.

"You go on up and change, Stanley," she said. "Tell Grant we'll be leaving soon. I'll see them to the door and be right up."

"Yes," said the senator. "No time to lose."

He shook Brendan's hand, patted Joshua and Heather on the head, and left the room.

"Poor Stanley," said Pauline, as they walked down the hall. "Always on the go. I keep trying to get him to rest, just every now and then. Slow down a little. But it's a hopeless cause."

"And you, Mother? How are you feeling?"

"Me? Strong as an ox. You know that. Never felt better in my life."

"Good. I'm glad."

She opened the front door and leaned down to kiss the children.

"Thank you so much for coming," she said. "Both of you. We had a lovely time."

"Thank you for lunch, Grandmother," said Joshua.

"Yes," said Heather. "Thank you for lunch, Grandmother."

Pauline smiled.

"You see?" she said to Brendan. "Perfect angels. Well, gotta rush."

She kissed Brendan and patted his cheek. "See you next time."

Brendan nodded, and she closed the door.

On the way home, Brendan asked, "How was your visit?"

"All right," said Joshua.

"The fried chicken was good," said Heather. "I liked that."

Their driveway was full of cars, and a number of others were parked along the curb. Brendan found a place in front of the Wilsons', two doors down. Heather held his hand as they walked toward the house.

Inside the front door, he could hear loud voices, laughter, and the clinking of cups from the direction of the living room.

"Will you two be all right in your rooms for a while?" he asked. "Marva's busy helping your mother."

"Sure," said Joshua.

Heather nodded.

"Come on, then. I'll take you up."

He got Joshua settled with his homework, helped Heather change her clothes and decide which dolls to play with, changed to jeans and a T-shirt himself, and went downstairs to his study. He closed the door, picked up the phone, and dialed.

"Jonathan? Thank God you're there."

"Why? What's up?"

"I just . . . have a desperate need for a little sanity."

20

The next week seemed particularly long to Brendan. Sandra talked about nothing but the success of her tea party. How gracious Deirdre had been to all the guests. A real lady.

Brendan called Jonathan every morning on his way to work, to find out how he was and to hear his voice, but wasn't able to see him. Wednesday night was Sandra's last committee meeting before the breast cancer ball on Saturday. Brendan had assumed he and Jonathan would be spending a few hours together, but, Sandra reminded him on Tuesday, that was also the evening of Heather's piano recital. She and the other beginning pupils. Brendan would have to take her.

Sandra was sorry. She'd had every intention of going as well, of course. But this meeting was too important to miss. They had to be absolutely certain everything was in order for the ball. Heather will understand, she said.

That night, onstage, Heather smiled brightly, curtsied like a champion, and charmed the audience, but played like an automaton. *All notes,* thought Brendan, *very little music.*

"Was I okay?" she asked on the way home.

"You were fine, sweetheart," said Brendan. "I was proud of you."

And he was.

He drifted through the rest of the week feeling uprooted, disconnected. His early-morning conversations with Jonathan were too brief, too impersonal, to relieve his sense of isolation. Making love to Sandra, so she wouldn't start wondering again, only made him feel more alone, not less.

On Saturday evening, he stood by himself on one side of the crowded ballroom. He watched the elegant, supremely confident people who filled the huge room, from mirrored wall to mirrored wall, elaborate bouquets of flowers towering above them. *They know they've arrived,* he thought, *and are thrilled to have a chance to let others know it as well.* Quite a few of them were dancing to the mellow music being played by the orchestra at the other end of the room. About half the local symphony, Brendan guessed. Others were standing in small clusters, eating, drinking, laughing.

The men looked very much alike in their tuxedos and black ties. Different sizes and shapes of men, but all in uniform. The uniform of success.

The women, though, were as determined to look unique as the men were to look the same. Their gowns—outrageously expensive, as Brendan was well aware—suffused the room with color. *No New York City monotony of black and pale ecru here,* Brendan thought with a smile. But nothing garish either. The reds were radiant. The blues deep and lustrous. The greens and purples soft and dusky. From everywhere—earlobes, necks, wrists—came the glittering sparkle of jewels.

He could see Sandra near the buffet table. She was in her element—and she looked it. Her mauve satin dress set off her piled-up auburn hair perfectly, the simple diamond clip that held it in place her only adornment. He had to admit she knew how to carry off this kind of thing.

So did he, of course. He'd grown up knowing how. He'd worn his first tuxedo at the age of six and had been to hundreds of these occasions since then. He hadn't minded most of them, had even enjoyed a few. This wasn't one of them. It all seemed too much.

He turned and saw Jonathan walking toward him. He looked magnificent, his dark skin making the black of his jacket and tie even blacker and the white of his shirt even whiter. Brendan felt his heart stop, then begin to pound. Until this moment, he'd thought that was just a romantic cliché. But it wasn't. His heart had actually stopped beating.

Jonathan smiled, held out his hand, and said, "Hello, Brendan."

Brendan shook his hand, was tempted to keep right on holding it, but let go.

"Hello," he said. "It's so good to see you. I hadn't expected you to be here."

"Nor had I. Then right after lunch I got an urge to see what all this was about. Lucky we singers have tuxedos in our closets. And . . . lucky there were still a few tickets available."

He looked around.

"So this is your world."

"Pretty much," said Brendan.

"Very glitzy."

"You seem to fit in quite well."

"Only because I'm dressed up and know enough to keep my mouth shut."

"What would you say if you weren't being polite?"

"Oh . . . that underneath this smile I'm heartsick—and a little angry. That one piece of jewelry on just one of these women would fund our clinic for a year."

"Come outside with me," said Brendan. "It's less overpowering out there."

A cool night breeze blew along the terrace. No one else was around. *All inside being seen,* thought Brendan. The French doors leading to the ballroom were open wide, and the music came out through them, clear and lovely. "Fly Me to the Moon" just then.

"I can't tell you how glad I am you're here," said Brendan as they walked. "I don't like it when we're out of touch, and today was . . . well . . ."

"It's good to see you, too. I wasn't sure, with such a crowd, if we'd be able . . . but this is fine. This is what I'd hoped for."

They reached the far end of the terrace and leaned on the parapet, side by side, looking out toward the river. Lights from buildings and bridges twinkled on its rippled surface.

"It's beautiful, isn't it?" said Jonathan. "At night like this."

"It is. And so are you."

Jonathan turned to look at him.

"If we were to go behind that row of azaleas," said Brendan, "no one could see us. What do you say?"

"I say, 'Follow me.'"

They walked to the other side of the large wooden planters, filled with thick green azalea bushes. Brendan leaned over and kissed Jonathan's mouth.

"Listen," he said, smiling. "That song from *Kismet*."

"'And This Is My Beloved.'"

Brendan held out his hand.

"Will you dance with me?"

"With the greatest of pleasure."

They put their arms around each other and turned slowly together in time to the music. Jonathan began to sing, quietly, near Brendan's ear.

"'*And when he moves, and when he walks with me, Paradise comes suddenly near!*'"

Brendan closed his eyes, transported by the sound of that deep, rich, pure voice and by the nearness of his—oh, yes—his beloved.

When the music stopped and Jonathan stopped singing, Brendan tightened his arms and said, "I love you. So much."

"And I love you."

After a minute, Brendan said, "Maybe we'd better go back in. We shouldn't stay out here too long."

"No, you're right. We shouldn't."

They walked back along the terrace and in through the French doors. Clarice came rushing up.

"*Here* you are," she said. "I've been looking all over. Out for a walk?"

"Yes," said Brendan. "And a little quiet."

She leaned over to kiss Brendan but stopped. "Oops. Better not do that." She winked. "But *you*, gorgeous," she said to Jonathan. "No one's going to stop me from kissing you."

She gave Jonathan's cheek a loud smack, leaving a circle of lipstick behind.

"What a pleasure to see you two together," she said. "I take all the credit for what seems to be a wonderful friendship."

Brendan smiled. "I'm happy to give you every bit of the credit. And yes, he *is* a wonderful friend."

"Didn't I tell you? But I'm taking him off with me now. The girls are all atwitter over how splendid you look tonight, Jonathan. Be a dear and come say hello. Give 'em a thrill."

Jonathan laughed. "How could I refuse?"

"As a matter of fact, you couldn't. But it's a lot easier if you come along willingly."

"Then that's what I'll do. See you around, Brendan. Call me when you have a chance."

"I will. I enjoyed our . . . chat."

Jonathan smiled. "So did I."

"Come on then," said Clarice. "Don't keep the girls waiting. Ciao, Brendan."

"Ciao."

She took Jonathan by the arm and led him away. Brendan watched until they disappeared into the crowd.

21

On the way home from church the next day, Sandra said, "I've been meaning to tell you. I had a nice talk with your friend Jonathan last night—stop hitting Joshua, Heather. You know better than that." She turned back to Brendan. "Ingrid reintroduced us, and I must say I liked him. Quite a lot."

"He's a very likeable man," said Brendan.

"The women flocking around him were certainly impressed. For good reason. I don't think I've ever seen a man look more stunning in a tuxedo. Well, you look wonderful, of course. Always have. But he . . . somehow he . . ."

"I know what you mean." *Do I ever,* he thought. "Maybe I'll drop by to see him this afternoon, if he's not tied up at his church. We didn't have much of a chance to talk last night, and I'd like to find out how he is and what he's been up to. I'll tell him what you said."

"Please do. Everyone likes to be admired. I'll be gone most of the afternoon myself. Did I mention that? Over to Lara's for a postmortem on the ball. Looks like it'll be our most successful ever. Close to four hundred thousand dollars, Lara thinks."

Brendan whistled. "Amazing."

"Not so very. We worked *hard* to make it happen."

"I know you did."

In Jonathan's bed that afternoon, Brendan couldn't stop holding him, kissing him, moving his hands over every inch of him. That first time, he'd felt surprise and a passion that was beyond his control. The second time was full of affection, ease, and a growing familiarity. This time was all love. He loved everything about Jonathan. He loved his face, his voice, his eyes, his smile. He loved touching him, feeling the strength of his muscles, the taut smoothness of his skin. He loved lying here beside him, breathing in rhythm with him, inhaling the air he had just exhaled. He was comfortable inside himself, in a way that was entirely new.

But then, from somewhere toward the back of his head, a feeling of uncertainty came creeping in. He was in uncharted waters here, out of his depth, and he had no way of knowing what to expect. Was he letting himself feel too much? They were so different in so many ways. What was it he had to offer that Jonathan might want? What assurance was there that he would keep on wanting it?

Jonathan snuggled in close beside him.

"You've gotten awfully quiet," he said. "What are you thinking about?"

"Us," said Brendan.

"What about us?"

"I was just wondering—why me?"

Jonathan laughed. "What a question! I don't know. Why *me,* for goodness sake? Do you know that?"

"No. Not really."

"Then, why should I?"

He lay quietly for a minute, then sat up and looked down at Brendan. "Still, since you ask . . . I do know *some* things."

"Such as?"

"Well, I know that I liked you the first time I saw you, there in your office. I liked the way you looked. And the way you trembled a little when you touched me."

Brendan blushed. "Oh, no. I was trying so hard not to. Hoping you wouldn't notice."

Jonathan laughed again. "Were you? Well . . . if I hadn't, we might not be here today."

Brendan smiled. "I certainly wouldn't want that."

"Nor would I."

Jonathan rubbed his hand across Brendan's chest.

"You are definitely none of the things I ever expected to be attracted to," he said. "I mean, look at you! White. Married. So often unavailable. Lots and lots of other men would've been far less . . . complicated. But I've met my share of them, and found it easy enough to pass them by." He moved his hand to Brendan's cheek. "Not you, though."

"Because?"

Jonathan frowned and lay down again in the curve of Brendan's arm.

"Because . . . one thing that keeps coming into my mind is that day at the clinic, when you rushed in to take care of Shantelle. It made me see you with new eyes. Before that, I'd thought of you as someone . . . different. Exotic. In a very exciting way, I have to say."

"*Me!* Exotic?"

"Of course. All that blond hair—and those blue, blue eyes. Like the sky on a cloudless day. Amazing. But . . . I don't know. Those were surface things. Things I could be attracted to, enjoy being around for a while, and then move on. What I began to see, that day at the clinic and afterward, were more solid things. Your decency. Your kindness. Your . . . what? Your generosity of spirit, struggling to get out from under great mountains of repression."

Brendan shook his head. "I wish I could see myself that way. The way you do."

Jonathan smiled. "There's a solution, you know."

"What's that?"

"Spend more time with me, and I'll help you see it."

"If only I could."

Jonathan shrugged. "You can do what you want to do."

"What do you mean?"

"I mean . . . life is full of choices, isn't it? And we end up choosing the things we want most. Simple as that."

22

Brendan had a full schedule on Monday, but he took some time out during the afternoon, between patients, to make a few phone calls. When he got home, he found Sandra lying on the sofa in the den, watching the news.

"Can we talk a minute?" he asked.

"Sure," she said. She aimed the remote at the TV and clicked it off. He sat in an armchair facing the sofa.

"I'd like to do some volunteer work at Jonathan's clinic," he said. "Every other Saturday—for continuity, I thought." He couldn't tell how she was reacting and decided he'd better just plunge ahead. "They're so woefully short of doctors down there. It's a pity, really. The need is enormous." He hesitated. "I do understand your concerns, though, so I talked with Ed Leverett, one of Arthur's partners at the law firm, and he says I'm protected from liability if I'm a bona fide volunteer."

Sandra nodded. "Good," she said.

"I've thought about it a lot since that day when I visited there. I really want to do this. We have so much, Sandra. I want to start giving something back."

She nodded again. "I can understand that. It's why I worked so hard on the breast cancer ball, and why I spend time, when I can, over at the hospital gift shop. Of course we can't just take all the time. But I . . . if you're *sure* you won't be running any risk of . . ."

"I'm sure. Ed Leverett read me the legislation. It's quite clear."

"Well, then, by all means. If it makes you happy."

Brendan called Jonathan the next morning, on the way to work. Jonathan was overjoyed.

"Brendan! What a wonderful thing to do. Twice a month? I'll just double my time there, too. So I can be there with you."

"I'd love that."

"So would I. Everyone at the clinic will be delighted. They think you're terrific."

Brendan laughed. "Let's hope I don't disappoint them."

"I can't imagine that."

"So will you be going this Saturday? I've lost track."

"Will you?"

"Yes."

"Then I will, too."

"May I pick you up on my way? Come up for a minute before we head on down? Give you a hug?"

"Oh, yes. Absolutely."

On Saturday morning, however, Brendan was late getting away from the house. Joshua had a question about his science project— a model he was building of a rocket motor—and Brendan ended up sitting on the floor with him in his room, trying to figure how best to fit two of the pieces together. By the time they finished, it was almost eight twenty. Brendan called Jonathan from the car, and he was waiting out on the sidewalk.

"Life keeps intruding," said Brendan, as Jonathan snapped on his seat belt.

"It does. But we're together now, and that's what matters."

Brendan pulled out into the line of traffic.

"How do you feel?" asked Jonathan. "Your first day on a new adventure."

"Excited. Also nervous in an odd way. I don't know why. I've been seeing patients for years. But not in a situation like this. I don't really know what to expect."

"People, Brendan. Parents, with sick kids. Worried about how they are. If they're going to be all right. That's what you can expect."

They arrived at the clinic just before nine. Many of those waiting in line outside waved and said hello to Jonathan. The pretty young Hispanic woman was at the reception desk.

"Hello, Doctor Garrison," she said, her hand over the receiver she was holding.

"Hello."

"Nice to see you again."

"You, too."

"I'd better get to work," said Jonathan. "See you later?"

Brendan nodded.

Nurse Proctor came up the hallway, smiling.

"Such a pleasure to have you here, Doctor," she said. "After your experience last time, I figured you'd either be hooked—or scared away for good."

"Hooked," he said.

"Well, I can't tell you how glad I am about that. How glad we all are. It'll be wonderful having you with us. Whenever you can fit us in. I know you'll be glad to hear that Shantelle's doing very well. She's gone to a shelter—one that takes in battered women—for a while. We're all thrilled about that."

"As am I. I hope she'll be all right."

"I expect she will."

"So there'll be another doctor here today, won't there? I understood there'd be two of us."

"That's what was supposed to happen, yes. Doctor Randall was scheduled to come."

"Paul Randall?"

"Yes. But when he heard you were coming, he called to say he thought he'd let you handle things, and come himself some other time."

"I see."

"You may be swamped, I'm afraid. When we thought we'd have the luxury of two doctors today, we called up a number of the mothers who've been waiting weeks to have their children looked at."

"Wait a minute. You haven't had any doctors here at all? For weeks?"

"Oh, yes. Most Mondays and Thursdays. But they don't like to come on Saturdays. Many of them don't want to cut into their weekends like that. Can't say I blame them."

"But if these children need medical attention, why don't their mothers go ahead and bring them in? On a Monday or a Thursday when someone's here?"

Proctor laughed.

"You do come from a different world, don't you, Doctor? The women I'm talking about all work, for bosses who don't have much patience with stories about sick children. No, Saturdays are definitely easier, even it if means having to wait for a while. Let's go on back now. We need to get you settled before the onslaught begins."

An onslaught it was. One child after another without letup. Measles. Strep throat. Diarrhea. Rashes. On and on they came. Sweet kids. Tough, hard-faced kids. One—a little girl, four and a half, her mother said—so lethargic and vacant eyed that Brendan became alarmed. He examined her gently, then looked up, frowning.

"Your daughter is seriously undernourished, Ms. Horton. If this goes on, the damage may be severe."

The woman's eyes filled with tears. "Oh, God. My baby! I been so afraid . . . I . . . oh, God! I try to get her to eat what we got, but she not interested, mos'ly. Just sit there."

He almost snapped at her, but stopped in time. What earthly good would that have done?

Just be calm, he told himself. *Think.*

What the child needed was hospitalization. Intravenous feeding for a while. Constant observation to monitor her progress. But that was impossible, apparently. He was out of his element here. Floundering. The things he knew to recommend couldn't be done. What else could he suggest?

"You *must* get her to eat, Ms. Horton. You *must*. Protein, especially. Calcium, and iron."

"I don' know what you mean."

"Meat. Milk. Cheese. Raisins."

"Milk make her sick. She throw up. An' I sure can't afford no meat."

"Why not? Aren't you working? I thought . . ."

"Was till Tuesday, when I sprain my back. Bad. But it gettin' better. Some. 'Nother few days I oughta be where I can start tryin' again. See what else I can find."

"Has anyone looked at your back?"

"Like who?"

"A doctor. A chiropractor even."

She laughed. "Now, how'm I gonna 'ford somebody like that? All we got's this place here."

It was a nightmare. Brendan felt as if he were sinking into quicksand with nothing to hold on to.

He picked the little girl up and put her on the chair.

"Please take your shirt off, Ms. Horton, and lie on your stomach on the table here."

He touched the stiff muscles of her back, up and down along her spine.

"Thank you. You can put your shirt back on."

He wrote on a prescription form and then on a piece of paper.

"Here are the things I want you to do. First, fill this prescription. It's for a muscle relaxant. It'll make your back feel better and speed your recovery. Next, buy these things for your daughter and see that she eats them. A little at first. Then more as she gets stronger."

Ms. Horton was shaking her head.

"You a good man, Doctor," she said. "I can see that. But you losin' your grip here. I been tryin' my bes' to tell you—I got *no* money. Not for no relaxers. Not for food. Not for *nothin'!*"

"Wait here for a minute, please, Ms. Horton," said Brendan. "I'll be right back."

He went out to look for Jonathan, who was sitting in the office working at one of the computers. Jonathan looked up and smiled.

"Bookkeeping," he said. "My least favorite thing. How's it going?"

"Wild," said Brendan, "but I'm hanging in there. I need your help."

"With what?"

"I've got a woman back there with a sprained back and a daughter who's suffering from serious malnutrition. I assume we can help her get the medicine she needs, but what about the food? That's just as important, as far as the little girl is concerned."

"I'm afraid she'll have to go elsewhere," said Jonathan.

Brendan shook his head. "Too complicated. Another place for her to have to go and wait? We ought to have some kind of fund right here, for emergencies like this."

"I suppose we ought to, but we don't."

Brendan reached into his wallet, took out three hundred dollar bills, and laid them on the desk. "Use this to get one started," he said. "I'll send a check next week to beef it up a bit."

"That's very generous of you," said Jonathan, "but I don't see how we can do anything before Monday. I'll have to call the director and see what she has to say."

"Do whatever you have to do," said Brendan. "Just get that little girl some food as quickly as you can. All right?"

Jonathan smiled. "All right."

Brendan started out the door, then turned back.

"One more thing," he said. "Find Ms. Horton a class on nutrition. That may do the most good of all."

"Yes, sir!" said Jonathan. He smiled again.

Ms. Horton and her daughter were waiting in the examining room.

"On your way out," Brendan said, "please talk with a young man named Jonathan Miles. He'll help you get the medicine I've prescribed and some food for your daughter. He'll also try to find you a class you can go to—where you can learn more about what your daughter needs to be eating. And you, too."

Ms. Horton stood up and reached for her daughter's hand.

"I wanna thank you, Doctor, for all you doin' for us."

Brendan nodded.

"I'll be here again week after next," he said. "You come back then, and bring your daughter. Let me see how you're both doing. All right?"

"All right. I don' know how to . . ."

"Just do what I've asked you to do. *All* of it. That's the best thanks you can give me."

A little before one, as a young man with bronchitis was just leaving, Gloria Ortega stopped in the doorway.

"Got time for a sandwich?" she asked.

"If I can eat it in here between patients," said Brendan.

She laughed. "Welcome to our world."

She brought him a ham and cheese sandwich and a glass of iced tea. He finished most of the sandwich and half the glass of tea before the next patient came in.

Brendan's three o'clock quitting time came and went. Three thirty. Four thirty. Quarter of five. The next time Proctor brought a patient in, Brendan stepped out into the hall with her as she left.

"Is Jonathan still here?" he asked.

"Are you kidding? He says he'll be around as long as you are."

Brendan smiled. "Please thank him for me. Would you call my wife, please? Tell her I'll do my best to be home by six thirty. Jonathan can give you the number."

"Do you want him to call instead?"

"No. I don't think so. You can tell her who you are. Make it sound official."

She laughed. "I hear you. Loud and clear."

They were out the door and in the car a little after five-thirty.

"We're cutting it close," said Brendan.

"Drive fast," said Jonathan. "This car can handle it."

"Let's find out."

On the freeway, as they headed uptown, Brendan asked, "What were you able to do for Ms. Horton and her daughter?"

"Get a few balls rolling at least," said Jonathan. "She'll have what she needs sometime early next week."

"Good," said Brendan. "I just wish we could've gotten her some food right away."

"Maybe next time we can. Sheila, our director, liked the idea of the emergency fund. Said to thank you for the 'seed money.'"

"Tell her she is very welcome."

"If I know her, she's already working on a plan—how much we should have on hand, criteria for deciding how much to give and to whom, and who will have the authority to distribute it."

Brendan wrinkled his forehead. Jonathan laughed and put his hand on Brendan's knee.

"Nothing's ever simple, you will find," he said. "Not even generosity."

As they turned onto Jonathan's street, Brendan said, "Well, once again, no time for ourselves."

"Yes, but look what you did with that time instead."

He squeezed Brendan's leg.

"I'm going up with you," said Brendan. "For a minute or two at least."

"I'd love it. Of course. But you'll never find a parking place. Not on a Saturday afternoon."

"I don't care. Let them give me a ticket. I'll tell them I was making a house call—which is the absolute truth."

Jonathan laughed.

There were no spaces. Brendan did double-park just down the street from the entrance.

Upstairs, he put his arms around Jonathan and held him as close as he could. Jonathan leaned his head on Brendan's shoulder.

"Do you know how much I love you?" said Brendan.

"I have a pretty good idea. And you?"

"I like to hear you say it."

Jonathan tightened his arms.

"I love you," he said. "I love you. I love you."

They stood there, close and at peace, for a minute or two. Then Brendan loosened his arms and moved back. He touched Jonathan's face and kissed him gently.

"Better go," he said.

Jonathan nodded. "Yeah."

"I'll be in touch. As often as I can."

"I know."

Brendan made it home in time for dinner. Just. He washed his hands on the way toward the dining room, kissed Sandra and the kids, waved to Marva, and sat right down. No one had started yet. *Thank God,* he thought.

Sandra smiled at him.

"So how was it today?" she asked. "A zoo?"

"Busy. *Very* busy. But fine. Nice people. I liked them."

"You managed to go all day without slitting any throats?" She winked at him.

He smiled.

"Yep. All day."

23

Another long week passed without Jonathan. Talking each morning wasn't nearly enough, and not seeing him made Brendan feel uneasy, out of sorts.

Now that the ball was over, Sandra turned her attention back to their own social life. That Friday evening, she invited Adele and Sam Reilly and Trish and Harvey Lundquist to their house for dinner. Sandra loved these occasions, small though they were. Planning the menu with Marva, ordering flowers, buying a new dress, having her hair done. Telling Brendan everything she was doing. On Friday, Brendan went through the motions—he liked Sam and Harvey well enough—but his mind was elsewhere. No one seemed to notice.

The next Monday, they went out for dinner and a movie with Lara and Dan Carmichael. Good dinner. Stupid movie.

Wednesday evening, after dinner at home, Sandra came into Brendan's study, where he was sitting in his big overstuffed leather chair, reading *The Bluest Eye*. It was so disturbing that he was having a hard time getting through it. Sandra sat in the chair behind his desk. He laid the book on his lap.

"I just talked to Mom," she said. "She and Dad want me to bring the kids for a visit again this year. As soon as school is out, they thought. Before it gets too hot out there."

"Sounds like a good idea to me. All of you had a nice visit last summer, didn't you?"

"We did, and it's time they saw the kids again. They won't believe how much Heather has grown. Well, both of them."

Brendan smiled. "No, they won't. I hardly believe it myself."

"You'll be all right here, won't you? All alone? Well, Marva will be here. To keep an eye on you. Cook your meals."

"I'll be fine. Of course I will. How long were you thinking of staying?"

"About two weeks, I'd say. That should be long enough for a good visit—but not so long they'll start wishing we'd go home."

Brendan smiled again. "Seems about right to me."

"Good," said Sandra. "I'll call Allison first thing in the morning. See what kind of flights she can find for us."

"I might even try to take a few days off while you're gone," said Brendan. "Relax around here a little bit."

"What a great idea. You could use some time to yourself."

That Saturday, on his way to the clinic, Brendan parked around the corner from Jonathan's apartment building—found a place just as someone was pulling out—and went up to get him, long enough to hold him for a minute, feel his closeness, feel the calmness his presence always brought with it.

Brendan was the only doctor on duty again, but the day was nowhere near as hectic as the last one had been. Many routine matters the others could handle, fewer serious ailments that demanded his attention.

Ms. Horton brought her daughter in. The little girl looked brighter, far more alert.

"I been feedin' her good," said Ms. Horton. "Foun' some things she like all right, from that class I took, so she eatin' better now. Thrill me to death."

"She certainly looks better. You're obviously doing the right things, I'd say. Congratulations. I'm very pleased."

Ms. Horton beamed.

"Now, how about you?"

"Feelin' better, too, more or less. Back's better—relaxer seem to help—so I'm workin' agin. Sweepin' up at a beauty parlor. Ain't much, but leas' we got money comin' in. Little bit. So I can't complain."

The afternoon passed smoothly, and he and Jonathan were able to leave soon after three. Their lovemaking was gentle and passionate at the same time. Afterward, they lay as they always did, Brendan's left arm around Jonathan, Jonathan's left arm across Brendan's chest.

Brendan felt a sense of being in exactly the right place. As if, after years of wandering, he had finally found his way home.

"Sandra's taking the kids out to Arizona early next month," he said, "to spend a couple of weeks with her parents in Scottsdale."

"And?"

"I was thinking . . . there are some cabins over at Lake Carson. If I rent one for a week or so, would you come out? Stay there with me?"

Jonathan sat up and looked down at him.

"Wouldn't that be lovely?" Jonathan said. "Days and days together."

"Could you get off from work?"

"I think so. Except for choir practice on Thursday night and the service on Sunday morning, of course. How far is it out there?"

"About an hour and a half."

"I could come out on Sunday afternoon. Drive in on Thursday and then go back out till . . . what? Saturday afternoon?"

"How about Sunday morning? You could get up real early, couldn't you?"

Jonathan laughed. "Yes, I could. Just think of all that time!"

"You like the woods? Hiking and being outside?"

"Love it. I grew up wandering around in the woods near our home. My sister and I were out there all the time. Chasing squirrels. Catching tadpoles. Listening to the birds. Trying to figure which was which by their songs."

"What's her name? Your sister?"

"Yolanda."

"Beautiful name."

"She's a beautiful woman."

"How could she not be?"

Jonathan smiled, leaned down, and kissed Brendan.

"You say the nicest things."

He settled back into the curve of Brendan's arm.

"What were you like?" asked Brendan. "As a little boy?"

Jonathan chuckled.

"Spoiled, mostly. Too cute for my own good. Everybody doted on me. Especially after I started singing in church."

"When was that?"

"The first time? When I was five, so they say. I remember the occasion vividly. It was before I started school. So five sounds right to me."

"What did you sing?"

"'Sweet Little Jesus Boy.' At the Christmas Eve service. In a starched white robe cut down to fit. Candles all around. I remember standing on a box so I could see over the railing of the choir loft. Just barely."

"Oh, my God. You must've been adorable."

"I'm sure I was. Of course, that very morning I'd probably been throwing rocks at Old Lady Evans's chickens. So I guess it all averaged out in the end."

"Were you a 'difficult' child, then?"

"Oh, I wouldn't go so far as that. I was inquisitive, let's say, and more than a little headstrong, which meant I did a lot of things that distressed my mama. But she was very forgiving. Strict—I had to stand in the corner a good bit, and went to bed without my supper a few times—but forgiving. She made sure I knew she loved me, even when I was being punished. Well . . . *especially* when I was being punished. 'This is for your own good,' she would say. And I'm sure it was."

"What about your father?"

"Papa?" He laughed. "The most easygoing man who ever lived. He'd try to do his part in making us behave—we were a rowdy bunch, all three of us. But he couldn't quite pull it off. He'd frown at us, and do his best to sound stern. But we knew his heart wasn't in it. We loved him so much, though, that we'd pretend to be remorseful and contrite. We'd promise him we'd do better. Even though we knew there was no chance we'd be able to keep that promise for very long."

"Did you ever get into real trouble?"

"Like with the cops? Or at school? No. I wasn't a bad boy. Just . . . lively. How about you?"

"Perfectly behaved. Always. Afraid not to be."

"Afraid?"

"Yes."

"Of your parents?"

"Of their disapproval. I wanted more than anything to make them happy."

"Which really means, make them love you."

"I suppose so, yes."

"Did they?"

"Oh, I'm sure they did. I never gave them any reason not to."

"So you assumed the responsibility for that? Keeping everything smooth and unruffled?"

"Yes."

"Couldn't it have been the other way around? Couldn't they have felt responsible for making *you* happy?"

"I guess they could have. But that's not the way it was."

"How about now?"

"The same."

"You've always been the one to make everything okay?"

"Yes."

"For everyone? Everyone *else?*"

"Yes."

Jonathan tightened his arms around him.

"Oh, my dear," he said. "That's the mountain I was talking about. Come on out from under it. Please."

Brendan closed his eyes and held him close. When he opened them, he glanced at the clock on the bedside table. Five seventeen.

"Got to go," he said. "Much as I hate to."

He kissed the top of Jonathan's head.

"I can't wait for our time at the lake—when I don't have to leave you like this."

24

The weather got warmer, and the days longer, most of them bright and clear. The occasional rainstorms were brief and refreshing. Brendan had the pool in the backyard cleaned and filled, and he started swimming a few laps after work, before dinner, on evenings when he got home early enough. Sometimes the kids joined him, splashing around in the shallow end. Sandra, who didn't like to get her hair wet or mashed down by a bathing cap, usually watched from one of the chaises, on the deck beside the pool.

The Memorial Day picnic at the country club was boring. Same people, pretty much. Same menu as last year, and the year before—hot dogs, hamburgers, baked beans, potato salad. The senator and Pauline were there, the center of attention, as always. Deirdre Beresford flew in without her husband and stayed with Sandra and Brendan for a few days. This time, Brendan's parents came for dinner at his house, and Sandra pulled out all the stops.

A week or so later, after the kids had finished school, they and Sandra left for Arizona on a Friday afternoon. Brendan drove them to the airport, kissed them good-bye, and drove back home. Marva served him his dinner in the breakfast room, and he went to his study to read.

Sandra called at about nine to say they had reached her parents' house. Her parents were fine, sent Brendan their love. He read till after ten, when Jonathan said he'd be home from the movies, called him to say good night, walked out by the pool to feel the breeze and listen to the crickets, and went up to bed.

On Saturday, he and Jonathan spent the day at the clinic, but skipped making love that afternoon, saving it for the cabin the next night. They had dinner at a little Thai restaurant near Jonathan's apartment building. Brendan walked with Jonathan to his apartment, kissed him, held him a minute, and went on home.

He was up early on Sunday, eager, excited. Marva made him pancakes for breakfast and kept insisting he have one more.

"I can't even imagine the kind of breakfasts you'll be fixing for yourself out there," she said. "Cold cereal, probably."

Brendan smiled.

"Probably," he said. "I hope you'll take it easy while I'm gone. Sit out by the pool. Jump in, if you feel like it."

She laughed.

"Can't you just see me doing that?"

"Well . . . ," said Brendan. "There won't be anyone here *to* see you, unless you invite them. So, help yourself. Do whatever you like. Just be sure to enjoy yourself."

She smiled and nodded.

"Thank you, Doctor," she said. "I appreciate the thought. You enjoy yourself, too."

"I'm sure I will."

Brendan arrived at the lake just after noon. He stopped by the general store to pick up the key and drove up a long dirt road to the cabin. It was exactly as the real estate agent had described it. Away from the lake, where the little houses along the shore were piled almost on top of one another. Off by itself, completely surrounded by woods.

He was pleased with everything. The porch out front, with its big wooden rockers. The rustic but comfortable furniture inside. The loft upstairs overlooking the living room, a queen-sized bed at one end and a large bathroom at the other. He tried the bed. Soft, yet firm. Perfect. He looked upstairs and down—no telephone, just as the agent had told him. *Good,* he thought. He'd had the brilliant idea, at the last minute, of leaving his cell phone at home, so there was no easy way for anyone to reach him. Or he them.

After he unpacked and put his suitcase on the shelf in the closet, he drove into town. He had lunch at the little café where he and Joshua had eaten, and came home with three bags full of groceries. He was sitting on the porch in one of the rocking chairs reading—he was about halfway through *Madame Bovary*—when Jonathan drove up a little after three. He got out of his car, and Brendan felt his heart stop, then race, the way it did each time he saw Jonathan.

He waited at the top of the steps as Jonathan waved, got a satchel out of the back seat, slung it over his shoulder, and walked toward him.

"Hi," said Brendan, smiling.

"Hi," said Jonathan. "Beautiful spot."

"It is, isn't it? I can't wait to go exploring. I've restrained myself till you got here."

"That was thoughtful of you."

Even though he was almost certain no one else was around, Brendan waited until they were up in the loft to put his arms around Jonathan, kiss him, hold him for a minute or two.

"We made it," said Jonathan softly. "We're here. Just us."

Brendan tightened his arms.

"Just us," he said.

He kissed Jonathan again and moved back.

"Come on downstairs when you've finished unpacking," he said, "and we'll take a walk in the woods."

"Great idea."

They found a path directly behind the cabin that went into the woods, up a little hill, and around to the right, away from the lake.

"Just look at these trees!" said Jonathan. "Almost as big as the ones back home. I had no idea there were trees like these in this part of the country."

Brendan smiled.

"They got saved just in time, I guess," he said. "When the state decided to protect all this. Good thing they did."

"I'll say. Imagine the loss if they were gone."

He went on up the path. Brendan was happy to fall behind so he could watch Jonathan walk, turn, look up, listen, smile. Birds were chattering and singing all around them. Sunlight broke, occasionally, through the branches, lighting up the path, the trunks of the trees, a few little yellow and pink flowers. The leaves above them fluttered, now and then, as a breeze blew past. The air smelled of dampness and rich earth. They saw no one on the path. *All over at the lake, no doubt,* thought Brendan.

Around a bend, they came to a stream, rushing along over its rocky bottom. Jonathan sat on the trunk of a tree that had fallen near its edge. Brendan sat beside him, close enough that their shoulders could touch.

"It's a wonderful sound, isn't it?" said Jonathan. "Water on its way to someplace else."

Brendan nodded. He wanted not to speak. He wanted to just sit here, listening to the stream. Feeling the breeze. Feeling the warmth of Jonathan's shoulder. His mind drifted. Leaves, sunlight, water. A sudden glint as sunlight bounced off water. Birds singing. An insect buzzing near his left ear. Jonathan beside him.

They sat a while in silence, leaning toward each other.

"Sorry to break the spell," said Jonathan, "but I'm getting hungry. Do you mind?"

"No. Not really. I am, too, now that I think about it."

They went back the way they came and were soon inside the cabin.

"I'm not a very good cook," said Brendan, "but I can manage stir-fry. Is that all right? Pork and some vegetables?"

Jonathan smiled. "Sounds great. I'll help, if you want me to."

"Do I ever. I can use all the help I can get."

They chopped, chatted, browned the pork in a skillet, threw in the vegetables and the seasonings. Jonathan stirred while Brendan set the table. As he was getting the plates out of one of the cabinets, he found two wooden candlesticks and a box of candles. He put two of them into the candlesticks and set them in the center of the table. He opened a bottle of wine Jonathan had brought, lit the candles, seated Jonathan, turned off the overhead light, brought the food over, and sat down. He reached under the table and squeezed Jonathan's hand.

"I love this," he said. "Us being here together."

"So do I."

Brendan poured wine for both of them, passed the bowl of stir-fry, and they began to eat.

"Delicious," said Jonathan.

"Mmm," said Brendan. "I guess it is. Miracles do happen."

Jonathan laughed.

"Have you heard about Shantelle?" he asked.

"No. Tell me."

"She's enrolled in a computer programming course at the technical college. Full scholarship."

"That's wonderful."

"*And,* she's booted that Conroy out of her mama's house and moved back home."

"Good for her. Have you seen her?"

"Phone call. Last night. She'd gotten my number from the clinic. Left a message, and I called her back. Said she'd thought about calling you, but decided she ought not to bother you."

"Too bad. I wish she had."

"She asked me to tell you how grateful she is, the next time I saw you. Said you not only saved her life, but changed it, too. Very much for the better."

"I'm so glad. She'll do well, I'm sure of that."

Brendan took away their plates and put vanilla ice cream and frozen strawberries into bowls, while Jonathan made coffee. Their conversation through dessert was easy and comfortable. The woods. The walk. The cabin. As natural, thought Brendan, as if they'd been doing this for years.

Jonathan washed the dishes, and Brendan dried them and put them away. When they'd finished, they went out onto the porch and sat in two of the rockers. Brendan couldn't believe how quiet it was. If there were nocturnal birds and animals nearby, they made no noise as they went about whatever they were doing.

"I love it here," said Brendan. "So much."

"Interesting that you do," said Jonathan.

"Why do you say that?"

"I've seen your house. I drove by one afternoon, just to take a look. It's an estate."

"Well . . . not quite."

"Looked like it to me. I've been wondering ever since what it must be like to live in a house like that."

"It's just a place. Bigger than some, I guess."

"Bigger than most."

"Right at this moment, there's nowhere I'd rather be than here."

Jonathan smiled.

"Good," he said. "Neither would I."

They rocked a while in silence.

"I checked out the shower in the bathroom upstairs," said Jonathan.

"And?"

"Plenty of room for two. Why don't we slip in there together, then head for the bed?"

The closeness of Jonathan's strong naked body, the touch of his hands as they soaped each other, the sound of his breathing, quick and excited—Brendan felt dizzy, disoriented, ready to burst with longing and desire. He turned off the water and reached for the big fluffy towels hanging there. They dried each other and moved, kissing all the way, toward the bed.

Their lovemaking was like the very first time—passion so intense it startled Brendan—but with an intimacy by now, a sense of familiarity, that filled him with tenderness.

Afterward, as they lay in each other's arms, Jonathan stretched and yawned.

"Sleepy," he said. "All this hiking and fresh air."

"See you in the morning, then," said Brendan.

Jonathan kissed him, settled into the curve of his arm, and was soon breathing smoothly and quietly.

Brendan's eyes, however, were wide open. He tightened his arms. What he felt most strongly was gratitude—for Jonathan, for being here with him. For the miracle of not having to leave. Time was what he'd been wishing for. Time like this—full and unhurried. Time for finding things out. He wanted to know everything he could. What Jonathan thought about when he was alone. What he hoped for, dreaded, disliked. What made him afraid. What made him lonely. What made him laugh. Everything.

These were thoughts Brendan was not used to having. Wondering what was down inside someone else—thereby moving, unexpectedly, far down inside himself. But he liked what he found when he was here, the person he was below the surface where he'd spent so much of his time. Down here, he was more aware, and he liked that. His only route to this place in the past had been books. Novels mostly. Poetry sometimes. They'd brought him here before, but he'd always thought of it as their place. The novelists' and the poets'. That he was just visiting. Now Jonathan had brought him here, and it was his place. His and Jonathan's.

Jonathan stirred, settled in closer to him, sighed contentedly, didn't wake. Brendan felt tears in his eyes and tried to blink them away, but they kept coming. Why were they coming? He was happy, wasn't he? Of course he was. But sad too. This place inside him was full of contradictions. Happy. Sad. Confused. Aware. Maybe his problem was that the place was almost completely unexplored. If he spent more time here, he would understand it better. He'd have to. He would keep coming back. He knew that now. He would come as often as he could.

He tightened his arms around Jonathan, closed his eyes, and hoped he could sleep. He felt at peace. Whole in that way he felt only with Jonathan. Maybe he *could* sleep.

And he did.

25

The next morning, Jonathan was still asleep when Brendan woke up. Brendan moved his arm out from under Jonathan's head as carefully as he could. Jonathan turned over and kept sleeping. Brendan dressed quietly, stopped by the bathroom, and went downstairs to see what he could do about breakfast.

He was reading the instructions on the back of a box of oatmeal when Jonathan came in, wearing a little light blue bathing suit, looking wonderful.

"It's going to be warm again today, looks like," he said, smiling. "The sun's out, and the sky is clear. So I went ahead and put my bathing suit on. Maybe we can go hop in the lake after breakfast?"

"I don't know," said Brendan. "I . . ."

Jonathan stared at him. "Oh, my God."

"It's just that . . . people might . . . I think we'll be better off if we don't—you know—attract too much attention to ourselves. I mean . . . two men spending time up here together."

Jonathan nodded.

"And one of them a black man," he said. "That would *really* make heads turn. Is that what you're saying?"

"No! That's not fair. I was just . . ."

"Come on. Don't try to duck this, Brendan. It's a fact of our lives. I'm black, you're not. Whenever we're together, people are bound to notice."

"Well, yes. But . . ."

"So what are our choices? If we don't want them to notice that—here, I mean—we'll have to stay in the cabin. Or only go into the woods, not into town. Correct?"

"Yes. Something like that. But . . . it's not that I don't want to be seen with you. You can't think that. We've gone places together, haven't we? In the city. Out to eat Saturday night. Remember? But here . . . I don't know. I want this to be *our* time. Just ours. Without other people's speculation about us interfering and making us—making *me,* anyway—uneasy. Worrying that they're looking at us and wondering. That's all I was thinking. Can't you understand that?"

Jonathan pressed his lips together, then nodded.

"Yes," he said. "Yes, I can. In the world I grew up in, you're the one who'd be conspicuous. You can bet everybody for miles around would be trying to figure out who you were. So . . . yes. Even though I can't help thinking there's more . . . No. Let's leave it at that. Yes, I hear what you're telling me."

He looked straight at Brendan, who couldn't think what else to say.

Jonathan narrowed his eyes, nodded again, and said, "All right. No swimming, then. I'll go change and be right back down. Can I help with breakfast?"

"Please. I think I've got the oatmeal figured out, and putting bread in the toaster is no great mystery, but maybe you could take care of the coffee again? What you made last night was much better than I've ever managed."

After they'd finished the breakfast dishes, they made sandwiches and put them, some fruit, and some bottles of water into Brendan's backpack, and headed out. A map Brendan had picked up on Sunday at the general store showed a network of trails. One went completely around the lake. Estimated time: six hours. Moderately difficult.

"Want to try that one?" asked Brendan.

"Sure. Why not?"

The day was beautiful. Warm, but an almost constant breeze off the lake kept it comfortable. They headed west, along the south side of the lake. Once it moved away from town, the trail went sometimes beside the lake, sometimes back into the woods. Most of the little lakeside houses, cabins, and boat docks were concentrated near the eastern end of the lake. Toward the west, where the terrain was rougher and the woods thicker, there were fewer houses, then none.

As the day wore on, Brendan was pleased to see that Jonathan's mood was improving, his basic equanimity rising through whatever it was he had felt earlier that morning. Soon, he was smiling again as he pointed at the things—trees, birds, views across the lake—he wanted to be sure Brendan had seen. They reached the far end of the lake and turned north, then back east. They ate their lunch sitting on a pile of rocks at the edge of the lake. Brendan couldn't remember when bologna and cheese had tasted so good. Or a simple bottle of water.

Just after one thirty, they came to a small clearing in the woods. Some marsh grass at its edge, then the lake. No houses. No boats. They'd seen no one on the trail all morning.

"Here's our swimming hole," said Brendan.

Jonathan turned, raised his eyebrows, began to smile.

"Without our bathing suits?" he said.

"I think we can risk it," said Brendan. "Don't you?"

Jonathan laughed and shook his head.

"You went to some lengths, I have to say, to get me naked in the water."

Brendan smiled.

"I'm just a sneaky guy, I guess," he said.

They took off their clothes and piled them beside a tree. Jonathan winked at Brendan, turned, and ran into the lake. Brendan ran in after him.

The water was perfect. Cool enough to be refreshing, warm enough that they could stay in as long as they liked. They swam out into the lake, floated, swam back toward shore. The sky was cloudless and very blue.

"Heaven," said Jonathan, as they sat in the shallow water. "Maybe it's a good thing, after all, that you were so nervous earlier. This is much better than being down there at the other end with the rest of the crowd."

"With our bathing suits on," said Brendan.

Jonathan laughed.

"Absolutely. That's the best thing about getting to swim over here. I love that feeling, don't you? Water touching you all over. It's so sensual."

"I'll say it is. Not that I've experienced it very often, outside a bathtub."

Jonathan shook his head again.

"Poor you," he said. "All those inhibitions. I'm surprised you don't explode, with all that bottled up inside you."

"Practice, I guess."

"I guess. Well, that's enough for me."

He stood up and walked out of the water. Brendan followed.

They lay on the grassy shore to dry off. Brendan propped himself on one elbow and looked at Jonathan, lying on his back with his eyes closed. His wet skin, deep rich golden brown, shone in the sunlight. Brendan felt a stirring between his legs.

Oh, no, you don't, he thought. He rolled over onto his stomach. Just being out here, naked like this, together, was brazen enough. They didn't dare do anything more.

Brendan heard a noise. Voices, growing louder. He sat up, panic rising in him.

"Someone's coming," he said. "What are we going to do?"

Jonathan sat up and looked around.

"Hide behind a tree," he said. "What else?"

They grabbed their clothes and ran toward the far end of the clearing. A huge log stretched from the shore toward the woods. They crouched behind it.

"Oh, look," said a woman's voice. "What a beautiful view. Look, Harvey. All the way across to the other side."

Brendan heard them walking. Away from him, it sounded like. Then he heard a deeper voice. A low rumble. He couldn't make out what the man was saying. The woman's voice again, farther away. Then nothing. He peeked up over the log. The clearing was empty.

"Well," said Jonathan. "That was fun."

"It was *not,*" said Brendan. "I felt like a naughty schoolboy."

"Good! It's about time. Apparently you missed out on being naughty when you were a kid, from what I hear."

"I did. Maybe . . . I don't know." He smiled. "I might be about ready."

They dressed, put on their hiking boots, and went along the path toward town.

26

Dinner that evening was spaghetti. Brendan heated up the jar of sauce, boiled the water, threw in the spaghetti, and kept tasting it till it was done just right. Jonathan made a salad—lettuce, carrots, celery, a couple of not-quite-ripe tomatoes. Some bread. More wine. Candlelight. The rest of the ice cream with their coffee. They talked about the day, the sunshine, the swim—across a divide between them that left Brendan feeling anxious and uncertain.

After they had finished the dishes, Jonathan went into the living room, turned on one of the lamps, and lay on the couch, staring up at the ceiling. Brendan sat in a chair across from him. He looked at Jonathan's face. The face he loved.

"It must be hard," he said. "Being black."

His boldness surprised him. He hadn't known he was going to say that.

Jonathan turned to look at him. Narrowed his eyes.

"Not quite," he said. He looked back up at the ceiling. "Being black is fine. I'm happy with that. It's who I am. The problem is what other people choose to make of that fact. What they see when they look at my black face. All of them have ideas about what this means. *Their* ideas. They see what they want to see, and then expect me to conform to that view, not my own. Be what they're willing to allow me to be. How crazy is that?"

He shook his head.

"Don't get me wrong, though," he said. "It's not that things aren't getting better. They are. I have to keep telling myself that. I've got it so much easier than my parents did. And we won't even talk about what *their* parents' lives were like. It's just . . . I get so tired. You know? Tired of other people wanting to define who I can be, and then if I won't be that, making it clear that I just don't fit in."

He continued to look at the ceiling, not at Brendan.

"That's one of the most powerful punishments society can inflict: shoving you outside the warm circle of their approval. They sit there, with their smug sense of entitlement, making the rules to suit themselves. The rest of us are supposed to do the fitting in. Well, I'm tired of it."

Brendan rubbed the back of his neck. "I wish I knew what to say."

Jonathan looked over at him. "What *can* you say? The fact is they're right. I don't belong anywhere. I don't fit into the world I came from. Not anymore. Not entirely. I sure don't fit into yours, as you so gently reminded me this morning. I'm not 'out' enough to fit into the gay world. But I'm not like other men, so I don't fit into the straight world either.

"Oh, I can fake it with the best of them. At church, and with those friends who would never understand. Dating some very nice women, but then having to make excuses for not taking them home to bed. I just . . . I get so tired of always having to . . . Isn't there any place where I can just *be?*"

"How about here?" said Brendan. "Right here. With me."

Jonathan smiled, shook his head, then nodded.

"Sure," he said. "This is great. Mostly. But we can't stay here forever inside this cabin. That leaves all the rest of the time."

"I don't understand. Why do you say you don't fit into 'my' world? What about the ball? You were surrounded by admirers. All those women. I couldn't get near you."

Jonathan shook his head—a bit sadly, Brendan thought.

"You really don't see things very clearly, do you?" he said. "They weren't admiring *me*. They were admiring the way I looked. Dark man, all dressed up fit to kill. I was like some kind of mascot. 'Isn't he cute?' And my, weren't they brave and liberated to be standing there talking to me? Smiling at me. Dancing with me, the most courageous of them. But admiring *me?* I don't think so."

"What about Clarice?"

"Clarice? She's very fond of me, I'm sure of that. Admires my singing. No question. Well, why wouldn't she? But she's never invited me to her house. She's not a friend, in that sense. I'm more of a . . . curiosity. That good-looking, talented Jonathan Miles. Quite a guy!"

He stared at the ceiling again.

"In a way, I prefer the racism of the South. There, at least, I know where I stand. Here it's more slippery, and that keeps me always a little off balance. I don't like that. I like a firmer footing. Less of a sense that I have to keep looking over my shoulder, never knowing where the next volley may be coming from."

"You sound angry."

"Do I? More like resigned, I'd say."

"So what can I do?"

Jonathan stared at him.

"Do? You can open your eyes for a start. See things. Really see them as they are. Not as you assume they are—or wish they might be. You are a very privileged man, Brendan. You've led a very privileged life. You're protected from the things I'm talking about by the color of your skin and by having a wife and kids—not to mention all that wealth that surrounds you. You don't have to be vulnerable unless you choose to be. It's up to you.

"For me, it's different. I'm just an ordinary guy, past thirty and still single. Plus, I'm black. I am judged the minute I walk into a room—or into a *lake*. I have to tell you—I want it not to be that way. I realize I'm asking too much. But . . . I want it not to be that way."

"Come upstairs," said Brendan. "Where I can hold you."

Jonathan looked at him steadily, then smiled.

"Is that always going to be the solution for us?" he asked. "When things get really uncomfortable, we can always go to bed? Well, why not? We aren't going to solve this tonight, or tomorrow night. Why not go do something more pleasurable?"

Once again, Brendan lay awake, with Jonathan asleep in his arms. But his feelings were far different from those of the night before. He remembered the old saying, "Be careful what you wish for." He had wanted to know what Jonathan thought and cared about. Deep inside himself. Now he knew. And knowing made him afraid.

27

The next days passed slowly, leisurely, but much too fast for Brendan. Jonathan did more and more of the cooking, something he was very good at. Brendan was delighted to let him.

Omelets for breakfast on Tuesday, followed by a walk in the woods behind the cabin. Tuna salad for lunch, followed by a nap. With all the windows open, upstairs and down, the loft was cool and comfortable. They lay on the bed in their underwear, holding hands. The tension of the night before seemed to have left them.

"I haven't taken a nap for years," said Brendan. "I can't remember the last time."

"Now, why am I not surprised?" said Jonathan.

Brendan laughed. "I suppose you have."

"Whenever I can. Naps are good. Usually, for me, they're short. Fifteen, twenty minutes. And I get up completely refreshed. Sunday afternoons in particular—after a long day at church. Just the thing."

Brendan was already feeling drowsy.

"I'm about to . . . ," he said.

When he opened his eyes and glanced at the clock, it was after two. He'd slept for more than an hour. Amazing. He turned to look at Jonathan, who smiled at him.

"Not bad for an amateur," said Jonathan.

Brendan laughed and stretched. "I think I could get used to this. Have you been awake long?"

"Not long. I woke up a while back, but the breeze felt so good I just closed my eyes and was gone again."

"Want to go back to our swimming hole?"

"You bet. With or without our bathing suits?"

"Without. I'm feeling quite daring, for some reason."

This time, they piled their clothes behind the big log and stayed longer out in the deep water. A group of hikers came to the edge of the clearing and waved at them. They waved back, and the hikers went away. They dried themselves with a towel they'd brought from the cabin, put their clothes on, and headed for home.

Taking chances isn't so bad, thought Brendan. *Once you get used to it.*

As they approached the town, Brendan noticed a sign that said Canoes for Rent.

"Do you know how to paddle a canoe?" he asked Jonathan.

"Absolutely."

"Could you show me?"

"I could."

"Then let's reserve one for tomorrow. What do you think?"

"I think I'd love it."

That evening, the chicken Brendan had no idea what to do with was transformed, by Jonathan's attentions, into coq au vin.

"Marvelous," said Brendan, after his third helping. "How'd you learn to do that?"

"My mama taught all of us the basics while we were young," he said. "Told us it was something we needed to know how to do."

"She was right," said Brendan. "And she taught you well."

After they finished the dishes, Jonathan wandered into the living room and turned on the little radio. Nat "King" Cole was singing "Mona Lisa." Jonathan lay on the couch. Brendan sat in the chair across from him. Next came Elvis. "Love Me Tender." Clearly an oldies but goodies program.

"If I were to close the curtains," said Brendan, "would you dance with me?"

Jonathan smiled.

"In a better world, I would dance with you straight down Main Street, but yes. Close them if you like."

Brendan pulled all the curtains tight, brought in the candles from the dining table, relit them, turned off the lamp, and took Jonathan in his arms. One lovely ballad after another. Patti Page. What was surely the Mantovani Orchestra. Even Pat Boone.

He held Jonathan tight against him as they moved slowly around the room. He felt more love for this man than he could possibly contain. It threatened to burst out of him and fill the room. Was he wrong, or had the unpleasantness of Monday morning brought them even closer together?

When that program ended and was followed by the wail of country and western, they turned off the radio, blew out the candles, and went up to bed.

The next morning, they put on T-shirts, shorts, and sneakers. After breakfast, on the way to get their canoe, Jonathan said, "I'm paying for this. All right?"

"Thanks anyway, but I can . . ."

"Of course you *can*. So can I. You said no to splitting the cost of the cabin, and had a houseful of groceries when I arrived, so I'm paying for the canoe. No arguments."

A middle-aged woman wearing glasses, her hair in a bun, took Jonathan's money, handed them two paddles, and showed them which canoe to take—a bright red one.

"Be back by five, please," she said, "so I can close up. Quarter till would be great."

"We'll be here," said Jonathan.

He put Brendan on the front seat and himself at the back. After only a few minutes, Brendan got the hang of the paddling, and they set off, heading west along the north side of the lake. Brendan could see right away that this was a wonderful way to travel—smooth, quiet, almost effortless. The canoe responded immediately to any change of direction, determined by which side of the canoe they paddled on and with how much force.

The woods along the shore glided by, serene and very beautiful. Brendan loved walking through them, but in a way, this was even better. The gentle lap of the water, the breeze their own movement created, the satisfying resistance in the muscles of his arms and shoulders as they pushed themselves along.

The sky was full of puffy white clouds, drifting aimlessly. Ducks swam near the shore, upending themselves from time to time to look for food beneath the surface of the water. Crows flew from tree to tree, cawing loudly. Brendan took off his T-shirt and let the sun beat down on his shoulders and back. The breeze blew gently across his chest.

They came to a small cove, pulled the canoe up onto the grassy shore, and ate their sandwiches and fruit, looking out across the lake.

"Happy?" asked Brendan.

"At this moment?" said Jonathan. "Very."

Brendan's shoulders were turning pink, so he put his shirt back on. They went a little farther along the lake, then turned around and headed back. They reached the dock by twenty of five.

When they got to the cabin, Jonathan told Brendan to go sit on the porch while he gave some thought to their supper. In a few minutes, he came out with a piece of paper in his hand.

"Mind driving into town to get a few things?" he asked.

"Of course not," said Brendan.

Jonathan handed him a list and a twenty-dollar bill. Brendan started to protest, but realized in time that he should not.

"I'll stay here and get things started," said Jonathan. "See you when you get back."

Talent and the things Brendan brought back from the store turned the ordinary package of hamburger meat that had been sitting in the freezer into beef Stroganoff.

"That was some meal," said Brendan. "Again. Do you cook like this for yourself?"

"I eat well, if that's what you're asking. I don't do elaborate things unless friends are coming over, but I like what I fix."

"So do I."

Jonathan smiled.

"Glad I'm able to help."

28

Dessert—tapioca pudding Jonathan had whipped up. Coffee. The dishes. Easy and comfortable, like the first night they were here.

Brendan was sitting in the living room reading—feeling the burden of Emma Bovary's unhappiness—when Jonathan came back downstairs. He was carrying a large, thick book. He sat in the chair on the other side of the lamp from Brendan.

Brendan looked up and asked, "What are you reading?"

"It's called *The American Opera Singer*. Fascinating. I've gotten as far as Mary Garden."

"She was quite a woman, I gather."

"Single-minded, certainly. She knew exactly what she wanted—and went out and got it."

"Have you always loved opera?" asked Brendan.

"Since high school. From the first time I heard it."

"Where was that?"

"At home. On the radio one Saturday afternoon." He set the book on the floor. "I was sick in bed, some kind of flu as I remember it. All by myself. My brother Alex was married by then, and Yolanda was off somewhere. Papa was working, of course. Mama was gone, too. Running errands, I suppose—shopping probably. Getting stuff she thought I needed or would like.

"I was tired of the program I'd been listening to. Who knows what? So I turned the dial around, and the most astonishing music started coming out. I'd never heard anything like it. People were singing in a language I couldn't understand, so I had no idea what was going on. But I could tell from the music that the woman singing was excited about something. Seeing the one she loved, it seemed to me.

"I was transfixed. There's no other way to say it. I was hypnotized by what I was hearing. I thought I'd never heard anything so beautiful in my life. A man sang. Then the woman again. All the time this orchestra rising and falling underneath them. I reached my hand over and rested it on top of the radio. To be as close as I could, I guess, to that music.

"Then the man and woman started singing together—an ecstatic duet. Gorgeous beyond believing. As soon as they had finished, the place erupted in applause, people shouting their approval. Pretty soon, a man started talking, telling the names of the singers who were coming back out to take their bows. I didn't know who any of them were. More applause. More shouts. More bowing. 'We'll be back after this intermission,' the announcer said, 'with Act Two of *Madama Butterfly*.'

"Well! I listened to every word that was said during that intermission. All about Puccini and the writing of the opera and how beloved it had become. When the announcer started talking again, I realized, to my great relief, that he was telling me what was going to happen in the next act. Butterfly has had a child and is waiting for the father to come back. And he will, she tells us. One beautiful day he *will* come back to them.

"The music began again, and I was even more engrossed because I knew what the people were doing. What they were singing about. Love and anticipation in the second act. Loss and betrayal in the third. But also steadfastness and sacrifice. Poor Cio-Cio-San. He *couldn't* love her, her Pinkerton. It wasn't allowed. So she had to die.

"The opera ended before anybody else got home. Thank goodness. I turned off the radio, glad no one was there to disturb me. I didn't want to hear anything else after that. Certainly not my sister or my mother talking about where they'd been. I just lay there, looking at the ceiling, my mind racing.

"It was such a gift. To have come to me like that. I couldn't quite grasp that human beings—people just like me—could actually *do* that. Those huge voices. Sound just pouring out. I thought then— right then—'I could do that.' And not only could I, I *should*. I'd been singing for years by then, and all of a sudden I knew. I knew what it was I wanted. I wanted to sing like that.

"No one else could understand it. My mama especially. That next Saturday, I was completely well, had been for days, but when afternoon came, I was right there by the radio. *Rosenkavalier* this time. Beautiful. *So* beautiful. That trio near the end was like angels singing. I could hardly breathe.

"As soon as I turned it on, though, Mama started getting after me. 'What are you doing inside here, son? It's a glorious day. Won't be so many more, soon as winter gets here. So go on outside in the sunshine.' 'No, Mama,' I said. 'Not today. I have to listen to this.' 'To what?' 'To this opera. Coming from New York City.' 'What are you talking about, child?' she said. 'That's white people's music. *Rich* white people's music. It's not for you and me.'

"'Yes, it is, Mama,' I said. 'It *is* for me. I love it.' 'Why?' she asked. A perfectly fair question, but I couldn't answer it. 'I just do,' I said, and she went away. Left me alone. But let me know, by shaking her head and clicking her tongue, that she didn't approve."

"Does she now?"

"Oh, yes. She's my biggest fan. Began to reconsider when she saw how serious I was about it. After I started taking lessons—from a teacher at a college nearby who listened to me sing and got excited. Mama couldn't help hearing me, practicing all the time, there at home. Little by little she started to pay attention, and to appreciate it. She's too good a musician herself not to. But even so, I'd say she's reached the point of liking it quite a lot. Not loving it the way I do.

"Still, for a while there, I kept wondering about that question of hers. Why care about this music written by a bunch of dead white men, whose lives couldn't have been more different from my own? But then . . . the more I learned about it, immersed myself in it, the less important that question seemed to be. The music had called to me, and I had responded. It was now a part of me. A thrilling, very satisfying part."

Jonathan stared at the far wall, his eyes shining, a smile pulling at the corners of his mouth. Brendan felt a wave of love for him and a bit of awe—at his willingness to embrace, not fear, something so all consuming.

"As time went by, I realized that not only was it a part of me, I was also a part of it. I saw how much I was bringing *to* the music. What I know. What I feel. What I am. It wasn't dead at all. It was just sitting there waiting for someone to give it life. We're collaborators, you see, the composer and I. He outlines it. I make it live. At those moments when I'm singing, I become all that this portion of the music represents. A person. His past, his present, his joy, his sorrow. Through me, through my interpretation, the music is set free—to become itself. To reach, as only music can, down into the souls of those who are listening. To touch *their* joys, sorrows. Loves, hates, fears.

"They were amazing men, these composers. They understood how melody can attach itself to emotion, then lift it up and carry it, soaring, to places neither of them could ever reach alone. I . . . I love their music. That's a fact. I love what it is and what it does, and what I have become because of it. And you know, this realization has made *me* free. Free from the tyranny of 'why.' All I have to do is love it. Sing it. Bring it to life. Not understand what has led me to it. Too much 'understanding,' I sometimes think, is bad for the soul. Brains are wonderful organs. They help us learn how to do things, what we ought to do and *not* do, what makes life better and what doesn't.

"But then, after the brain has done its work, we need to turn it off. Give it a rest and listen to our hearts. The brain brings us order and reason and discipline. All necessary—in their place. But it's the heart that gets us in touch with love and beauty.

"Think of flowers—peonies and roses and daffodils and lilies. Orchids, for heaven's sake. What earthly good are they, if you're not a bee or a hummingbird? What do they do, really, that people need? Not a thing. Except make this a world I want to live in.

"Music is the same for me. It doesn't *do* anything. Except make my heart—and my life—overflow with beauty. Not a bad reward, I'd say."

"Show me," said Brendan.

"Show you what?"

"What you're talking about. I love it, too, so . . . sing for me. Please."

"Now? Here?"

"Yes. Can you think of a better place?"

Jonathan smiled. "No." He stood up and walked to the far end of the room.

"I can't stand too close," he said. "I've got too much . . . power."

He bowed his head and touched both hands to his forehead. He dropped his hands, raised his head, and began to sing. In Russian. Brendan recognized it immediately. Onegin's lament for Tatyana— the woman he might have loved but didn't. And now realizes he does, with a passion that torments him.

Brendan was stunned. He felt as if he couldn't move. With his voice alone, Jonathan was bringing to life Onegin's world—a world of desire and anguish, love and despair. *Yes,* thought Brendan. *Yes, I see.* He was not just singing notes. He was using them to create something much larger than themselves. Brendan imagined the neighbors, even miles away, stopping what they were doing. Turning their heads to listen.

He'd heard opera all his life. He'd heard this kind of richness and depth before, but never such purity. Pure melody. Pure passion. Pure beauty. The sound of that extraordinary voice filled not just the air around him, but all the spaces inside his body as well. The room—and everything in it—*was* music.

Then he stopped. Too soon.

"I . . ."

Brendan wanted to speak, to tell him. But he couldn't think of any way to say what he was feeling. The whole room had become music? He couldn't say that. Instead, he got up, went over, and put his arms around Jonathan. With the curtains wide open.

"You were . . ."

Jonathan hugged him close.

"No need to explain," he said. "I could see it in your face."

29 🎵

Jonathan got up early the next morning, made French toast for breakfast, and washed the dishes while Brendan dried. He went upstairs and came down carrying a small briefcase.

"Leaving so soon?" asked Brendan.

"'Fraid so. I have quite a lot to do before choir practice tonight. Meetings, and some phone calls I need to make. But I'll drive straight back out afterward. Be here by eleven. Eleven thirty maybe?"

"I'll be waiting up for you."

"If you get tired, you could always . . ."

"Not a chance."

Jonathan smiled.

"Good," he said. "I'll be eager to see you, I'm sure of that."

"Me, too."

"Anything we need that I could bring out with me?"

"Well, another bottle or two of wine would be nice. Just in case. Oh, and some of those packages of mixed nuts and dried fruit to take with us when we go hiking—or better yet, canoeing. Shall I reserve one again for tomorrow? We could go the other way around the lake."

"Great idea," said Jonathan. "The thought of that will keep me going all day."

"But wait," said Brendan. "Will you have time to get those things, or will you be too . . . ?"

"I'll have time."

He put his hand on Brendan's cheek.

"I'm going to miss you," he said.

"And I you."

Brendan kissed him and held him close.

"You know how much I love you," he said. "Don't you?"

Jonathan tightened his arms. "I do."

He kissed Brendan once more, picked up his briefcase, and went out to his car. Brendan waved from the porch as he drove away.

The day was not as awful as Brendan had feared. He was lonely, but also full of anticipation for the time they still had left.

He got out his little map and took a trail that looped into the woods along the north side of the lake. He met three groups of hikers as he went, more people than they'd seen all week. *Must be because the weekend is coming,* he thought. He felt a bit as if his paradise were being invaded, but he smiled at them anyway. Most of them smiled and said hello in return. He stopped by to reserve a canoe for the next day on his way back to the cabin.

He had two bologna sandwiches, a few grapes, and some ginger ale for lunch. A nap, during which he tossed more than slept. He knew he was in no mood for *Madame Bovary,* so he took a *National Geographic* he found in a magazine rack in the living room out onto the front porch. He rocked and read until dinnertime. About the mysterious ancient city of Teotihuacán. The promise of sustainable agriculture. Young stars being born within the Orion nebula. He sat alone at the table with heated-up leftovers and a glass of wine. No candles. He tried making himself some coffee, but it was such a disaster he poured it all down the drain.

After he'd washed the dishes and left them in the drainer to dry, he got a flashlight out of the closet by the front door, flipped on the porch light, and walked down the dirt road into town. He thought about the brightness of the stars—where was the Orion nebula anyway? About Jonathan. About the canoe trip tomorrow.

The little houses along the lakeshore were all lighted up. A row of them stretched from one side of the lake to the other. So close together they almost touched. He heard dishes clattering, loud laughter, children shrieking, the sudden revving of a boat motor. Coming in, or going out? He had no idea and realized he didn't care. He wanted to be away from this noise and confusion. He headed back up the road toward the cabin.

He turned on the radio and lay on the couch. All the windows were open, and a breeze—pleasingly fresh but not quite cool—blew gently through the living room. "Some Enchanted Evening" was playing.

Ezio Pinza? Sounded like him. Then "Bali Ha'i." Then "Younger Than Springtime." The soundtrack from *South Pacific*. A special tribute this evening to Rodgers and Hammerstein, the announcer said. A young woman with a syrupy, slightly nasal voice.

"Coming up—*The King and I*. The movie version this time, starring Yul Brynner and Deborah Kerr. Right after these messages."

Brendan had a great time humming along: "I Whistle a Happy Tune." "Getting to Know You." The next song, though, struck him like a blow to the chest.

We kiss in a shadow; we hide from the moon. Our meetings are few, and over too soon . . .

Oh, no, thought Brendan. *No, no, no.* He felt a tightness in his throat and a stinging in his eyes. *I should be trying to figure out what on earth I'm going to do,* he thought. *I really should.*

But a talk show came on and distracted him. Creationism versus Darwinism. The way the host said "theory" when he talked about evolution left no doubt as to where his sympathies lay. His views were soon reinforced by most of the listeners phoning in. Something like ten to one in favor of the biblical account, it seemed to Brendan.

What about all these fossils, though? asked one caller, an old man clearly not used to talking to such a large audience. Proven, scientifically, to be millions of years old. What about that? Put there by Satan, the next caller assured him, in a vain attempt to discredit the works of the Lord God Almighty. But people of faith, whose trust does not waver, can see right through this clever ruse. See it for what it is.

Brendan looked at his watch. Ten after eleven. Jonathan would be here soon.

More talk. This time about pornography on the Internet. What parents can do to monitor the things their children are seeing.

Eleven thirty. Quarter of twelve. Brendan felt a twinge of concern. Where could he be? For the first time all week, he was sorry he'd left his cell phone at home. Did Jonathan have one in his car? He didn't know. And he certainly didn't know the number. Hadn't thought to ask.

More chatter about pornography. Brendan was becoming very uneasy. Just after twelve fifteen, he heard a car coming up the road. Then another.

Who else could it be. . . ? he wondered.

He turned off the radio and went out onto the porch. Jonathan's car had stopped near the steps. Behind it was a car with SHERIFF written in large letters across its side. Jonathan got out of his car—he seemed to be all right, so Brendan's initial surge of alarm began to ease a bit—and came to the bottom of the steps. Brendan went down to meet him.

"Are you . . . ?"

Jonathan shook his head, his face impassive.

A man in a khaki uniform—short, stocky—walked over from the second car.

"Your name Garrison?" the man asked.

"It is. And yours?"

"Akers. Deputy sheriff. This man claims he's staying here. With you."

"'Claims'? Of course he's staying here with me."

The man looked around.

"So . . . you renting this cabin from the Fergusons, then?"

"From a real estate agent, yes. Why?"

"What brings you here?"

Brendan felt irritation, verging on anger, rising in him. He fought to keep it down. He glanced at Jonathan, who was staring at the trees. He turned back to the deputy sheriff.

"Vacation," he said. "A restful time by the lake. Or so I thought."

"And this other fella? Why's he here?"

Brendan wanted to hit him, but merely clenched his fists instead.

"Jonathan is my friend," he said. "He's visiting me. Has been since Sunday. Was he speeding? Did he run a stop sign in town?"

"No."

"Well, then . . . was there an accident? Did his car break down?"

"Not that I know of."

"Then why are *you* here?"

"To check out his story."

"His story! Which you heard how? By pulling him over?"

"Yes."

"For no reason?"

The deputy narrowed his eyes.

"I had plenty of reason. The safety of this place—outside the park—is my responsibility. Dusk to dawn. I needed to know what he was doing out here this time of night."

Brendan glanced again at Jonathan. He was still staring at the trees. He seemed not to have moved.

"It's quite simple," said Brendan. "He drove into town earlier today. To lead a choir rehearsal this evening at his church. As soon as it was over, he started driving back out here, where he's been staying, to spend the night."

"Church, you say?"

"Yes."

The deputy's eyes shifted to Jonathan, then back to Brendan.

"Well," he said. "I guess it's all right then. But you can't be too careful. Not these days."

"Now that you've been 'careful,'" said Brendan, "may I assume that you are satisfied?"

"S'pose so. But I'll be . . ."

"You'll be what?"

"Nothing. I'll just say good night now, and be on my way."

Brendan nodded. Jonathan remained silent.

The deputy got into his car, backed up to turn around, and drove away. Jonathan walked, without a word, up the steps and into the cabin. Brendan followed him and slammed the door.

"Christ!" said Brendan. "That was the most outrageous . . ."

Jonathan turned to stare at him, his eyes hard, his mouth a tight line.

"Please, Brendan," he said. "Spare me your indignation."

"What?"

"I'm tired. I'm angry. I'm . . . let's just get some sleep. All right?"

"But can't we talk about it?"

Jonathan laughed. A harsh laugh that made Brendan wince.

"Talk about it!" Jonathan shook his head. "And say what? You're sorry? You love me? I know that. But I'm . . ."

He took a deep breath.

"I'm going upstairs to bed. You can do what you like."

Jonathan was on his side of the bed, facing the wall, when Brendan turned out the light and got in beside him. He moved over and put his arm around Jonathan.

"Don't do that," said Jonathan. "Not right now."

"Please," said Brendan. "I just want to . . ."

"Make it all right? Well, you can't. So let's just try to get some sleep."

Brendan took his arm away, rolled over onto his back, and stared at the ceiling.

30 ♪

On Friday morning, when Brendan woke up, the other side of the bed was empty. Jonathan was gone. Panicked, Brendan pulled on a pair of shorts and ran downstairs, through the living room to the kitchen. Jonathan was standing beside the stove, dressed in slacks and a sport shirt, stirring a pot of what looked like oatmeal. Brendan could smell coffee brewing.

Jonathan turned.

"Morning," he said.

He didn't smile. His eyes, always so warm and open before, were closed off. A curtain had been drawn between them, and Brendan couldn't see through.

"I was so frightened," said Brendan. "I thought you'd left."

"I am leaving. Right after breakfast."

"But *why?* We've got all day today—and tomorrow. That's what we planned. What about our canoe trip?"

"I'll be sorry to miss that." He stirred the oatmeal again. "But I can't stay here. Not now."

"Why, Jonathan? I don't understand how you could let a . . ."

Jonathan looked at him, his face hard.

"Are you deaf?" he said. "As well as blind? Are you really able to ignore *everything?* First I can't swim here. Not around other people, at any rate. I'd attract too much attention. Then they start wondering why I'm here at all. I don't belong in this place. That's the simple truth. I just don't belong."

"What are you saying? Of course you do. You belong with me."

Jonathan turned off the burner under the oatmeal.

"No, Brendan," he said. "I don't. I thought I did. I *wanted* to think I did. But I've been shown, quite forcefully, that I don't."

"Because some redneck fool let his prejudice get the best of him, you turn away from me? That's not fair."

"Fair?" Jonathan shook his head. "Only somebody in your position could even consider the possibility that life might be fair. Sit down. Eat your breakfast."

He poured two mugs of coffee, spooned oatmeal into two bowls, put them on the kitchen table, and sat in one of the chairs.

"Come on," he said. "Eat. It'll get cold."

Brendan sat across from him.

"I don't want to eat," he said. "I want you to stay. Who knows when we'll have an opportunity like this again?"

Jonathan set his mug down.

"That's the rest of the problem," he said. "Don't you see? We're here because you've managed to squeeze me into your full and very busy life. There you are, with your wife, your kids, your convertible, your fancy-dress balls. I'm just somebody you fit in around the edges, when it's convenient. When your wife's out of town—or off at a meeting. I thought I didn't mind. But I was kidding myself. I do mind. I'm worth more than that, Brendan. A lot more."

"Of course you are. I know that better than anyone. But what can I do? I have responsibilities. Obligations. I can't just . . . can I?"

Jonathan sighed.

"No," he said. "Why should you?"

"There's no reason we have to let all this come between us. Is there? I love you. You love me."

Jonathan nodded.

"True. But there are some things I know about love, and one of them is this: If it's going to last, mean something, it can't be just a romantic fantasy. The kind we've been playing at. You can't keep it tucked away in a little compartment and bring it out only on special occasions. When you've got time for it. It has to be out there all the time, gaining strength, so it can survive the harsh realities it's bound to bump up against, day after day. It has to—or it will die."

"Please, Jonathan. I can't bear this. Talking about things dying, when we've been so happy. I just want . . ."

Jonathan's face softened, a little. His voice was gentler.

"You want everything to go along exactly as it's been. You want things to appear to be just fine—no matter how much ignoring you have to do along the way. Well, you can't ignore what went on last night. That man was an asshole, and he treated me—*me*—like dog shit. There was nothing you or I could do without making it much, much worse. That's the truth. Pretending . . . ignoring . . . they won't work. Not this time. Nothing's going to make that ugliness go away."

"No," said Brendan. "You're right. Of course you're right."

Jonathan nodded.

"I'm not in much of a mood for oatmeal," he said, "so I think I'll just get going. There are the things you asked for. The wine and the nuts. I've left them for you on the counter."

Brendan felt tears again. Somewhere deep inside his eyes.

"Nothing I can say will make you stay?" he asked.

Jonathan shook his head. "Nothing."

He took one last sip of coffee, stood up, and walked into the living room. Brendan followed. Jonathan's satchel was beside the front door. The sight of it grabbed at Brendan's chest.

Jonathan turned, put his arms around Brendan, and held him close.

"I still don't understand," said Brendan.

Jonathan moved back, put his hand on Brendan's cheek, smiled. A sad, rueful smile.

"Think about it," he said. "See if you can work it out."

He kissed Brendan, picked up his satchel, walked though the door and down to his car.

31

Brendan dumped the oatmeal into the garbage, left the dishes to soak, and headed down the road toward town. He took the fork that went along the north side of the lake.

He kicked at rocks as he went. Wished he could pick them up and smash something. He was angry with Jonathan. Furious at him. How *dare* he ruin their plans? Leave like this, without giving them a chance to . . . What kind of love was that anyway, that wouldn't even . . . ?

Then he remembered what Jonathan had been through, tried to imagine what it must have been like, and his anger shifted immediately to the deputy sheriff. What a moron that man was, that he couldn't tell the difference between Jonathan and some . . . some what? Some young black hoodlum? Who ought to be stopped?

There it was, thought Brendan. Plain as day. His own subtle racism, tucked away inside him, that let him feel outrage for Jonathan but not for all the others who spent their lives dealing with this kind of harrassment. As this realization began to sink in, his anger shifted once more, onto himself.

So much anger—and no good place to put it.

He turned off the road and walked down to the dock where the rental canoes were tied up. He told the woman to cancel his reservation. He wouldn't be going out after all.

"If you think you might want one for tomorrow or Sunday," she said, "you better tell me now. Things get pretty hectic around here, summer weekends."

"Thanks, anyway," said Brendan. "But that's not going to be possible."

The next days were bleak and lonely. Bright sunshine and clear skies seemed to mock him. So did the laughter of the people he passed, on the trails and in town. At the store and in the little café. Everything was empty for him now. The woods. The cabin. The big queen-sized bed.

He was angry. Sad. Confused.

He felt at loose ends, rattling around with no purpose. Several times he decided to just give up, pack his things, and go on home. Then he would think, no. That would be even worse. Marva clucking over him, asking what was wrong. Why he'd come back sooner than he'd expected. So he stayed—and each time, before long he was sorry he hadn't left.

Back and forth. Back and forth. But one thing was constant: an overpowering need to be in touch with Jonathan. Yell at him. Apologize. Just say hello. Something. Anything. He kept walking into town to call him from the pay phone outside the general store. Friday afternoon. Friday night. Four times on Saturday. Always the machine. He left messages only twice. Casual ones, fit for public consumption. He didn't know who might be around. Friends or . . . whoever. He didn't want a bunch of lovelorn pleadings recorded there, for anyone to listen to.

When he woke up on Sunday, the last thing he wanted to do was leave the cabin, with all it had meant to him. After breakfast—corn flakes, no coffee; he'd given up even attempting that—he wandered back into the woods, as far as the stream they'd found that first afternoon. He sat for more than an hour on the log, staring at the rushing water.

He was supposed to be out of the cabin by noon. He finally left at quarter till. He drove a little way down the road, stopped, turned to look back at the cabin, then drove on. He left the key at the general store, had a bowl of soup at the café, and took the long way home around the lake and through some beautiful farmland. He put the top down on the convertible, in order to enjoy as much of the scenery as he could. Corn tall, healthy, leaves a dark, vivid green. Houses tidy, well cared for. Large barns. Silos. A few cows and horses here and there. Bright blue sky.

When he reached the city, a little after three, he put the top back up, closing himself in. He drove straight to Jonathan's apartment building. Surely he'd be home from church by now—but he wasn't. Brendan rang the doorbell ten, fifteen times. No answer.

Downstairs, he sat for a long time in his car. *Might as well go on home,* he thought. But he didn't want to. He didn't want to be there. He didn't want to be anyplace where Jonathan wasn't.

At last he drove home. As he walked through the front door, carrying a suitcase and a bag of leftover groceries, Marva came toward him down the hallway from the kitchen.

"Here you are," she said. "I heard you drive in. I was wondering if you'll be wanting to have your dinner here tonight."

"Yes," said Brendan. "I will. I'm ready for some of your cooking, I can tell you that."

Only true since Jonathan left, he thought.

She smiled. "I appreciate that, Doctor. Is six-thirty all right?"

"Fine. Thank you. I'll go shower and change."

"Oh, a young man brought a letter by for you. Nice-looking, polite young black man." He heard the unspoken question in her voice. "I put the letter on your desk."

"When did he come by?"

"About an hour ago, hour and a half."

"Thank you, Marva. I'll see you at six thirty."

She took the bag of groceries from him and walked toward the kitchen. He went out to his car, brought in his other suitcase, and carried both of them up to his bedroom.

He wanted to know what the letter said—and he didn't want to know, in case it was something final. Not wanting to know was stronger, so he put off finding out. He went to the phone on Sandra's night table and called Arizona. Her mother answered. "So nice to hear from you, Brendan, she said. "It's lovely having them out here with us. Here she is."

"Hi, honey," said Sandra. "Back from the lake?"

"Yes."

"How was it?"

"Beautiful. Restful."

"Did you do any fishing?"

"No. But I did make it out in a canoe."

"A canoe! Well, why not? We're all having a great time, of course. The kids have been swimming at the pool here every day. Joshua's been taking diving lessons. He's very good. Oh, and we've been out to the . . ."

She chattered on about what they'd been doing. Where they'd gone. Whom they'd seen. Friends of her parents mostly. Not many other kids around, kind of a shame, but Joshua and Heather were bearing up. Brendan only half listened. Once she'd slowed down and stopped for a breath, he said, "You'll be home on Saturday, then?"

"Afternoon. Around three fifteen. The flight number and exact time are on the bulletin board in the kitchen."

She started in again, about a cocktail party. Who was there. What they'd served.

"Let me talk to the kids a minute," said Brendan.

"Of course. See you Saturday afternoon. Don't be late."

"I won't."

Joshua talked about his diving lessons, Heather about a new dolly her grandma had given her.

After he hung up, Brendan thought again about the letter and was still hesitant to read it. He started unpacking instead. He showered, shaved, put on jeans and a T-shirt, and finally went back downstairs to his study.

On his desk was a sealed envelope. He took it over to his reading chair, sat down, turned on the lamp, and opened the envelope.

Dear Brendan,

I got your messages, and was happy to hear your voice, but didn't know how to call you back. You didn't say. I was out a lot on Friday and yesterday, making arrangements and getting ready for an unexpected trip.

I'm leaving this afternoon for San Francisco. I have an audition tomorrow with the opera company there. My voice teacher at Mannes, a strong supporter of mine, knows some people who say they're interested in hearing me. He's been after me for a while to go on out, but I've been putting it off because of you. Because of us. Now I think it's time to go.

I know I'm taking a chance writing this letter, but it seems safer and more private than a phone message. I am trusting that you will be the only one who sees it. With that hope in mind, I will tell you that I love you, more than I can say. You are dear to me in ways nobody else has ever been. But too much out there in the world is against us, and won't let us be. There's nothing either of us can do about that, that I can see. The best thing, I think, is for me to try to find a place for myself, and for you to go back to where you already belong.

I will always be grateful for having known you—and having loved you. I wish things could have been different, but they're not.

Think good thoughts for me tomorrow. I'll be in touch as soon as I get back.

With all my love,
Jonathan

Brendan folded the letter, leaned his head back, closed his eyes. He was far too sad for tears.

32

Monday and Tuesday were full, busy days for Brendan. So many patients to see. Regular appointments, plus some of those postponed from last week. He worked through lunch and till after six both days, grateful for such an effective distraction.

Late on Tuesday evening, around ten, he was in his study listening to *Turandot*. Calaf had just struck the gong, signaling his acceptance of the Princess's challenge, when the phone rang. Brendan put the CD player on pause and answered.

It was Jonathan.

"I hope it's all right to call," he said. "At home, I mean. And so late. I forgot till I'd already dialed about the time difference."

"Are you kidding? Of course it's all right. How'd it go yesterday?"

"Very well. Very, very well. My first audition was such a smash, apparently, that they called me back in this afternoon for another. So some more people could hear me. They're almost ready to say yes, but there are a couple more steps they have to go through before they can. Checking schedules and contracts and things like that, from what I gather. I could know as early as the end of this week. First of next week. Can you believe it? I can't tell you how excited I am. It's like a dream. I never thought it possible."

"You didn't? Then you're the only one. No one who's ever heard you would be the least bit surprised. I'm certainly not."

"Are you happy for me? I mean, assuming it works out."

"Oh, it will. They'd be insane not to grab you. And yes. Of course I'm happy for you. Heartbroken in a way, but also very happy."

"Thanks, Brendan."

"When will you be home? Do you know?"

"Late on Wednesday. Tomorrow. In time for choir practice on Thursday. I'll have to start seeing what I can do about finding a replacement. Just in case."

"What time does your plane get in?"

"Eight forty-five. Around there."

"I'd love to meet you at the airport. May I?"

"Could you? That would be great."

Brendan was waiting outside the security area on Wednesday evening. Jonathan came toward him, smiling. Brendan shook his hand, patted his shoulder.

"You look terrific," said Brendan. "California must agree with you."

"San Francisco does, certainly. It's a wonderfully open city. I loved it there. I only have this carry-on, so we don't have to fool with baggage claim."

"This way, then."

Inside the car, Brendan leaned over and kissed Jonathan.

Jonathan smiled.

"It's good to see you," he said.

"You, too," said Brendan.

He started the car, backed out, and headed for the exit.

"Have you eaten?" he asked.

Jonathan laughed. "Not much. You know what their 'snacks' are like. Have you?"

"No. I waited for you, assuming you'd be hungry. That little Thai place all right?"

"Perfect."

Their conversation through dinner was mostly about Jonathan's trip. The auditions. The people he'd met. Where he'd stayed. The weather. He'd had lunch at a marvelous sushi restaurant where the diners sat around a long oval table, with a space in the middle where the chefs did all their chopping and rolling and shaping. A narrow moat filled with water ran around the inner edge of the table. The chefs standing in the center placed dishes of sushi on tiny wooden boats that floated around the moat past all the diners, who reached over and took what they wanted. Each diner made a stack of the col-

ored plates the sushi came on, the cost of the item being determined
by the color of its plate.

"Lots of fun," said Jonathan. "And really delicious."

"Who took you?"

"Some people from the opera company. Nice people. Warm. Wel-
coming."

They made love gently, quietly, and lay without talking in each
other's arms for a while.

Brendan looked at his watch. Nearly midnight.

"I'd better go," he said. "Another busy day tomorrow. For both of
us, I'd guess."

Jonathan nodded.

"May I call you in the morning, on my way in?" asked Brendan.
"Our old routine. Will you be up?"

"Yes, I'll be up. I'd like that very much."

33

Brendan's call to Jonathan on Thursday morning was brief, frustrating. It seemed to have nowhere to go. Brendan felt sadder and lonelier after he called than before, but was still glad to have talked with Jonathan. These were the last remnants of something beautiful that was ending, and he was determined to hang on as long as he could.

Friday morning he asked if they could do something together that evening, and Jonathan said no.

"I have a long-standing engagement for dinner with friends. I haven't seen them for a while, and they're eager, especially now, to catch up on all my news."

"Couldn't you postpone it?" asked Brendan.

There was a silence at the other end of the line.

"Your family's coming back when?" asked Jonathan.

"Tomorrow. Midafternoon."

"And you were hoping to spend this last evening with me. While you still can."

"Yes."

"So here we are. Right back where we started. I guess the answer is, yes, I could postpone it. But I don't think I will."

"I see. But . . . I can call you again Monday morning?"

"Of course."

"And you call me, please—home, office, anywhere—if you hear anything before then."

"I will."

Their plane was right on time. So was Brendan. He kissed Sandra and the kids, gathered up their luggage, and drove them home in the Jeep. The three of them talked excitedly, Sandra most of all.

It was great, they all agreed. Just long enough, said Sandra. Mom and Dad aren't as young as they used to be—well, who is?—and two kids for too long gets to be wearing. So . . . just long enough.

After they got home, Brendan made sure to spend time with each of the kids alone. He read to Heather for a while before dinner. A new book her grandpa had given her, about a Pueblo Indian girl. He spent almost an hour in Joshua's room after dinner, talking about his trip to Arizona, his diving lessons, his plans for the rest of the summer. Joshua asked if Brendan had liked being out at the lake. Brendan said yes.

He found Sandra in the den downstairs watching television. She clicked off the set and started in again. The visit hadn't all been rosy, by any means. She was concerned about her mother. Forgetfulness and repeating things. She asked her father privately if they'd seen a doctor about it, and he acted as if he didn't know what she was talking about. Very worrying. She'd have to figure a way to do something, force the issue from here, which wouldn't be easy.

She asked about Brendan's trip, and he told her the things she was interested in hearing.

"Was the cabin nice?" she asked.

"Yes. It was."

"Nice furniture?"

"Very comfortable."

"Did you cook for yourself?"

"Sometimes. Not every meal. There was a café in town. Where Joshua and I ate that day."

She laughed. "I'll bet you were a regular customer."

"Not really. You'd be surprised. My stir-fry and spaghetti weren't bad."

She went back to fretting about her mother. What if it really was Alzheimer's? Her dad would never be able to cope. Her mother was the one who'd always held things together.

Brendan tried to listen—to care—but his heart wasn't in it.

After they'd gone to bed and turned out the lights, he and Sandra made love, and it was fine. His thoughts were of Jonathan, not Sandra, and he felt guilty about that at first. Then didn't.

34

Church on Sunday morning. Lunch afterward with the senator and Pauline. Another complete retelling of the Arizona trip. Dinner and a long, quiet evening at home. A call to Jonathan early on Monday. Again on Tuesday.

Later that day, around midafternoon, Jonathan called Brendan at his office. Brendan was with a patient, but called him back as soon as he could.

"I just heard a little while ago," said Jonathan. "They've offered me the position in San Francisco. And I've accepted."

"Of course you have," said Brendan. "It's wonderful. But I . . ."

"I know."

"When will you go?"

"Right away. The man I replaced at the church, who retired when I came here, is willing to take over again for a while. Till they can find a permanent replacement. Says he can start as early as next week, so . . . I guess there's no reason to put it off."

"No," said Brendan. "I guess not."

"Which makes me think—the sooner the better. I'll need to find an apartment. That isn't easy out there, they tell me."

"How soon?"

"Next Monday. I just confirmed my reservation."

"Oh, dear God."

"I was able to find a reasonably inexpensive fare on the Internet. Very handy, that."

"But . . . Monday?"

"Yes. They want to give me a big farewell at church on Sunday. They were so confident they started planning it as soon as I got back. I'll wait for that, then go on out."

"This is very hard for me," said Brendan. "I . . ."

"Me, too. Please believe that. Me, too. But it's what I've always wanted. Well, for years and years. Now that it's here, I can't wait to get started."

"I can understand that."

"Can you?"

"Well, sort of. Will I have a chance to see you before you go?"

"Oh, yes. I mean, as far as I'm concerned, yes."

"What's best for you?" asked Brendan. "Maybe dinner on Saturday night? Just the two of us?"

"That would be great. Can you manage it?"

"Wild horses couldn't keep me away."

"Good. I'm glad. Saturday night for dinner it is."

"And our phone calls? Every morning between now and then?"

"Absolutely. I'll count on them."

As they were getting ready for bed that evening, Brendan said to Sandra, "Jonathan Miles has been offered a position with the San Francisco Opera. He's leaving next Monday."

Sandra smiled. Was there relief in that smile? Brendan thought so, but he couldn't be sure.

"That's very good news," she said. "Please give him my heartiest congratulations."

"I will. I'd like to take him out for dinner on Saturday. Give him sort of a send-off. Any conflicts I'll have to deal with?"

"None. And I think that's a lovely idea."

Yes. Relief was definitely hidden there, somewhere.

On Saturday, Brendan spent the day at the clinic. Jonathan did not. He had far too much to do before Monday.

Brendan picked Jonathan up at seven, as arranged. Jonathan looked magnificent in a well-cut deep blue suit, white shirt, maroon paisley tie.

"New suit?" asked Brendan.

"New everything," said Jonathan. "Like it?"

"Very much."

They were going to the Lion d'Or, a French restaurant over by the river. The most expensive place in town. Jonathan had objected. Brendan had insisted.

Brendan ordered Veuve Clicquot champagne.

"You don't have to impress me," said Jonathan. "You really don't."

"That's not why I'm doing this. I just want you to know that, as far as I'm concerned, only the very best is good enough for you."

Jonathan smiled.

"Well," he said. "That's all right then."

Their conversation was awkward, frustrating for Brendan. The calm easiness that had always been there between them was gone.

Afterward, as they were drinking their coffee, Brendan felt a hand on his shoulder.

"Two of my favorite people," said Clarice.

Brendan and Jonathan stood up.

"Wonderful to see you," said Jonathan.

"Hello, Clarice," said Brendan.

She leaned over and kissed Jonathan.

"I've heard your marvelous news," she said, "and I couldn't be happier. You'll be sensational."

Jonathan smiled. "I hope so."

"Hope so! My dear, they're the lucky ones. When do you leave?"

"Monday morning."

"Heavens! So this is your farewell dinner."

"Yes."

"You're going to miss him, Brendan. I can guarantee you that."

Brendan nodded. "You're telling me."

"Well, my dears. I'd better be getting back to my friends. Ernestine and Michael Forsythe, Brendan. And Rob Huntington, the old rascal. He's being very attentive these days."

"As well he should," said Brendan. "Tell them all hello for me. And be sure to let me know if Rob becomes more than just attentive."

"I will," she said. "Indeed I will." She laughed, a little too loudly. "Sandra would be thrilled to hear it, I'm certain of that."

"Thank you so much for coming over," said Jonathan. "I've enjoyed knowing you, and . . . I'll miss you."

"You, too. You have my e-mail address. Let me hear from you after you get settled."

"I will. You can count on it."

Clarice leaned over and kissed Jonathan's cheek, smiled at Brendan. She put her hand on his arm.

"You know," she said, "I hope Rob *does* propose. Then I can kiss you in public safely again."

Brendan smiled. "I'll look forward to that."

Making love with Jonathan back at his apartment was as awkward as dinner had been. Brendan had wanted it to be extraordinary, like the first time. Memorable. It wasn't.

They said good-bye at the door, Brendan in his suit, Jonathan naked, beautiful.

Brendan held him close.

"It seems impossible to me that this is happening," he said.

Jonathan tightened his arms. "Well, it is. But don't forget: we've had a hell of a ride."

Brendan nodded. "Yes, we have. Hook up your e-mail the second you get out there, all right? Let me know how to reach you."

"You know I will. As soon as I can."

Brendan kissed him again and left.

35

Those next days passed slowly for Brendan. His work was routine—nothing unexpected or complicated. He and Sandra chatted, went to a cocktail party, watched TV with the kids.

Joshua was pursuing his diving with gusto. Taking lessons at the country club. Practicing every afternoon, he told his father proudly, in their pool out back. Most evenings, before dinner, he had something new to show Brendan. He *was* good. Heather had given up her piano for the summer, preferring to spend her days with her friends.

Each hour, by itself, seemed interminable, but together, somehow, they continued to pass. Brendan managed well enough. Habit took over from feeling—and he managed. He smiled at people, was pleasant to everyone, the way he'd always been, but mostly he felt empty inside.

His regular Saturday at the clinic was the closest he came to his old life. A little after eleven on a not particularly busy day, Nurse Proctor put her head in the door. She smiled.

"Someone to see you, Doctor," she said. "I'll hold the next patient for a few minutes."

Brendan looked around as Shantelle walked through the door. She held out her hand. Brendan squeezed it and, before he realized what he was doing, leaned down and kissed her cheek.

"I hope I'm not disturbing you," she said.

"Never."

"I brought my aunt by to have her blood pressure checked, and they said you were here. So I thought I'd say hello."

"I'm delighted you did. It's such a pleasure to see you. You look wonderful."

"Do I? Well . . . my life's good. Maybe that's it."

"You're at the technical college, I heard. Computer programming, is it?"

"Web site design. That's what I like best. The creative part excites me."

"And what about your life? The rest of it."

"Never been better. I've found me a gentle, kind man. Treats me like a princess."

"Because that's what you are."

She laughed.

"The princess who came back from the dead," she said. "My own version of 'Snow White.'"

Brendan smiled.

"With me on your side instead of a bunch of dwarfs."

She laughed again.

"I'll take you. But . . ." She shook her head. "How I can ever thank you enough?"

"By staying in touch. Whenever you can. Letting me know how you are. We have a special bond, you and I. I don't ever want to let it go."

She ducked her head.

"Thank you, Doctor," she said. "I appreciate that."

He reached for a pad of paper.

"Here's my cell phone number," he said. "You can always reach me there. Call as often as you like. Especially when something good has happened to you. Graduation. New job. Whatever. Will you do that?"

She smiled. "Yes. I will."

"Promise?"

"I promise. Well, I'd better let you get back to work."

"Probably. This was a lovely surprise. I'm counting on you to keep in touch. And to make a huge success of your life."

"The life you gave me. Good-bye, Doctor."

"Please give my regards to your mother."

She laughed. "Indeed I will."

36

More days crept by. Still no word from San Francisco. Brendan was worried, but what could he do? He had no idea how to reach Jonathan.

The senator's big Fourth of July party was a welcome diversion. The social event of the summer. Every summer—without fail. It had never rained that Brendan could remember.

What he remembered best was that the parties were always the same. Festive. Suitably patriotic. But always the same. Mountains of catered food served in tents on the broad, carefully tended lawn behind the house, from midafternoon on. Liquor flowing. Crowds of people milling around, laughing, eating, drinking. Celebrating their independence. Younger children running and shrieking. Older ones doing their best to look grown-up.

This year, as always, the cream of local society had gathered there. No one would think of missing it. Dignitaries had flown in from all over. Governors. Other senators. Congressmen. Party leaders. The Beresfords, of course, who were staying with Sandra and Brendan.

Jock Rawlings, everywhere at once, promoting his race for Congress. Clarice, wearing a huge diamond ring. Rob Huntington had, in fact, proposed. Quite suddenly. Wedding sometime in the fall. She kissed Brendan right on the mouth.

In the largest of the tents, a dance band played till after dark, when the fireworks began. More than half an hour of color and explosions filling the sky. *Amazing,* thought Brendan wryly as the show got under way. They were illegal in the rest of the county—private fireworks. Not in the senator's backyard.

As soon as Brendan got home, he went to his study to check his phone messages, then his e-mail. A note from Jonathan was there.

So sorry I've been out of touch for this long. I thought I'd have a phone number, or at least an e-mail address, much sooner, but it's been frantic. I've been hopping around, staying with different people from the opera company, like a vagabond. Now, though, as of yesterday, I have a place of my own—a tiny apartment, but I love it. On the third floor of a Victorian row house. No elevator, of course! That'll help keep me in shape. Lots to tell you. Here are addresses, home and e-mail, and my phone number. Call me?

Jonathan.

It was only eight-thirty in California, so Brendan tried the number. Jonathan answered.

"Thank goodness," said Brendan. "Not off watching fireworks someplace?"

"I could have been," said Jonathan. "But I decided I'd like to stay home for a change. Now that I have a home to stay *in*."

"You've been going out a lot?"

"Quite a lot. Too much, really, for my taste. Everyone's being so friendly and eager to introduce me around."

"Where have you been going?"

"Dinners at people's apartments most nights. A number of them gay, as it's turned out. Which has usually meant a trip to one gay bar or another afterward. Very freeing and fun. A bit wearying sometimes, but fun. Like the old days in New York. And I do love to dance."

"Then you're meeting lots of gay men?"

"Oh, yes. They're everywhere."

"Does that mean . . . ? I don't quite know how to ask this, but . . . is there a romance in your life?"

Silence for a second or two.

"I don't mean to complicate your life, Brendan. Any more than it already is. But I don't see any point in not telling you the truth. In spite of the difficulties we've encountered—and all the miles between us—you are the romance in my life. I know very well I'm going to have to find somebody else to care about. I mean, I'm not going to spend the rest of my life alone. But not now. Not for a while yet."

"I'm glad to know that. Even though there's nothing I can do about it, I'm still glad. I just . . ."

"It's all right," said Jonathan. "Believe me. It's all right."

37 ♪♫

That Thursday, late in the afternoon, Brendan was with a patient. A woman in her early seventies here to check on how her new arthritis medication was doing. He heard a faint knock, and Cathy stuck her head in the door.

"I know you don't like to be disturbed, Doctor," she said, "but your father's on the phone. Says it's urgent."

"Tell him I'll call him right back."

"I tried that already. He says now."

Brendan took a deep breath.

Don't snap at her, he thought. *It's not her fault.*

"Thank you, Cathy," he said. "Tell him I'm on my way." She eased the door shut. "I *am* sorry, Mrs. Melrose. I'll be back as soon as I can."

"Don't you worry, Doctor," she said. "I'll be right here."

He walked out of the examining room, closed the door behind him, and went directly to his office.

"Father?" he said. "Is Mother all right?"

"Of course she is. How pressed are you right now?"

"Winding down. I'm with a patient—almost finished. One more after that. Why? What's up?"

"Well, get rid of them quick and come on over here. We need to talk."

"About what?"

"Jock Rawlings has had a stroke. Sometime this morning. Your mother and I just got back from the hospital. He's pretty bad. Paralyzed all down one side. He'll live, they say—we can all be grateful for that—but there's no way he can go on with his campaign."

"You want to talk with me about his condition?"

"No, for Pete's sake. You can be such a dolt sometimes. About your taking his place. Running for Congress."

"Me?"

"Of course you. Don't act so surprised. We've talked about it a hundred times. Practically since you were born."

"But . . . now?"

"When Fate opens a door—spreads it wide like this—you rush on through it. You bet your sweet life, now. Besides, it's the best way the party's got of being certain we win this race. New candidate so late in the game—only three months left. It's essential we have someone with real name recognition. And you know as well as I do there's no name in this state more recognizable than mine—and therefore yours."

"Wait a minute," said Brendan. "You're moving too fast. I'll need some time to think about this."

"You'll need no such thing. Time is exactly what we don't have. Finish up what's left to do—don't dawdle—and get on over here. Your mother will call Sandra and tell her to meet us here. We'll start filling you both in on what has to be done, and when."

A click, and he was gone.

Brendan reached his parents' house a little after five. Sandra was already there, and the three of them were sitting in the senator's office. Brendan sat in the chair across from his father.

"Drink?" said his mother. "Before we get started?"

"A glass of wine would be nice," said Brendan. "Whatever you've got."

His mother started toward the bar. His father was already talking.

"I'm still having a hard time believing our good fortune," said the senator. "Couldn't be a better year for you to run for the first time. We're right on all the issues—dead on target. The political climate around here is dependably conservative, and people seem to be pretty well satisfied. Not looking for a change to begin with. So what kind of alternative are they being given? A self-avowed liberal. An idealistic tree hugger! The fool Democrats are practically offering it up to us on a platter."

His mother handed him a glass of red wine, kissed the top of his head, and sat down. Sandra smiled at him. He smiled back. He knew how thrilled *she* must be.

"Now," said the senator, "for some specifics. I'll spend tonight and all day tomorrow on the phone. Filling people in. Rounding up support. Putting a campaign team together. Difficult, with so many of the best people already committed.

"Then I'll have to get started on finding the money we'll need. *Lots* of it these days. Luckily we can count on most of Jock's supporters to just shift right on over to us, but I've got some other people in mind as well. IOUs it's time I called in, and plenty more, waiting in line, who'd like nothing better than a chance to do me a favor."

Brendan glanced at his mother. She was listening intently, a half-empty martini glass in her hand.

"We'll want quite a bit of TV time, of course," the senator continued. "As much as we can afford. Saturate the district with your face—your family's faces. Being so attractive, all four of you, is a godsend. Guaranteed to warm the hearts of every voter in sight."

He looked over and smiled at Sandra. She smiled and nodded.

The kids? thought Brendan. *He wants us to use the kids?*

"So," said the senator. "You see why I wanted you over here right away, Brendan. No time to lose. Not a second. Everything's breaking in our favor, but we've got to do all we possibly can to capitalize on that. Call on the wealth of political savvy your mother and I have built up over the years. Give this race every ounce of energy and enthusiasm we've got. Go out there and crush the opposition. Make her wonder what hit her. Make her wish she'd never even bothered to run in the first place."

Brendan stared at his father with grudging admiration. *I see now,* he thought, *why no one's been able to defeat him for forty years.*

"You two go on home," said the senator. "Do whatever talking you have to between yourselves. Plan on showing up here again Saturday morning for a strategy session. Nine o'clock, say? No, better make it eight thirty. Get a running start on the day. We'll have a breakfast of some kind for you here, so don't take time for that. Just come on over. We'll get our thoughts together—the four of us—before we start dealing with everyone else. Best if we have an absolutely united front here in the family. And, of course, I'll be able to fill you in on what all I've gotten done between now and then.

"We won't be announcing your candidacy until Monday. Decent interval after Jock's misfortune. Don't want it to look as if we're leaping into his grave, so to speak."

The senator stood up. The rest of them did, too.

"So that's our game plan," said the senator. "You go do what you need to do. Your mother and I will get right to work from here."

Dismissed, thought Brendan.

He shook his father's hand and kissed his mother. Sandra kissed them both and started through the door. The senator and Pauline were seated again, deep in conversation, before Brendan was out of the room.

Sandra had taken a cab over so they could drive home together. On the way, Brendan shook his head.

"I don't remember saying yes," he said. "But it looks like it's an accomplished fact. No way to stop that steamroller now."

"Good heavens!" said Sandra. "You weren't actually contemplating saying no, were you?"

"I guess not. In fact, now that I'm over the initial surprise—I guess 'shock' is a better way of describing it—I'm beginning to see how exciting this could be. I'd miss my practice, of course, but I keep thinking of the things I know something about that could be handled so much better. I've been thinking about them a lot these past few months—becoming more and more concerned. Now here's a chance to actually do something constructive. Make a difference. Assuming I win, of course."

"Do you have any doubts?" asked Sandra. "With your name? And your parents behind you? We might as well start looking for a house in Washington. Which, I have to say, is the exciting thing for me. Living there. Georgetown, I think. And just *being* there. Right at the center of things. Deirdre says the social life is quite astonishing. Non-stop. Parties, dinners all the time. She says a lot of the business—maybe most of it—is conducted at social occasions. So while you're off in a corner saving the world, I'll be having myself one heck of a time."

38 ♪♫♪

Brendan couldn't wait to get home so he could call Jonathan. Sandra headed for the kitchen to talk with Marva about dinner, and Brendan went right to his study. Jonathan's machine answered. Too early out there—only late afternoon. He decided not to leave a message.

During dinner, they told Joshua and Heather.

"I've seen them on TV," said Heather. "People wanting to get elected. Will we be on TV?"

"Yes, sweetheart," said Sandra. "We will."

"All of us?"

"Yes."

"Do I get to talk? Or do I have to just sit there?"

Sandra laughed.

"I'm sure you can say something sometimes. If you want to."

Heather nodded.

"I'll show you the dress I want to wear on TV."

"How about you, Joshua?" asked Brendan. "How do you feel about it?"

"I'm not sure," he said. "Is it really going to happen?"

"Your grandfather seems certain that it will, yes."

"Then . . . will we have to move?"

"For most of the year. We'll be back here during the summers. But Washington is an interesting city. I lived there for a while when I was young."

"That means . . . I'll have to go to a different school."

"You will," said Brendan. "But you'll make new friends. The other kids will like you there, the same way they do here."

"What if . . . ? If I don't want to go?"

"You don't have that choice," said Sandra. "Sometimes things happen in life that we didn't expect, and we just have to make the best of it."

Brendan put his hand on his son's arm.

"Don't be afraid," he said. "That's the important thing. I was when I was your age, and I wish now I hadn't been."

Joshua looked away, then back at his father.

"There'll be pools, won't there?" he said. "With diving boards? Somewhere close by?"

Brendan smiled.

"Of course there will."

As soon as they finished, Brendan went back to his study to try again. This time Jonathan answered.

"That's terrific news," he said. "You'd make a marvelous congressman. You're smart, caring, sensitive. Don't forget courageous. I've seen all of that in action. I'd say you're just about perfect for the job."

"Sure you can't come back for a couple of months—to work on my campaign? Go around telling other people what you've just told me?"

Jonathan laughed.

"'Fraid I can't, though I would dearly love to. But it's not as if those things are a big secret. Other people are sure to notice and line up in droves to vote for you. What are your chances, do you have any idea?"

"My parents seem to think it's no contest. That all I have to do is show up."

"Well, I'd have to respect their judgment about that. Be sure to keep me posted on how it goes. All the details. I've never been this close to a political race before."

"I have, of course," said Brendan. "Lots of them through the years. But this is different. This is *me*."

"Are you nervous?"

"A little. But also eager. You know?"

"I do know. And I'd say hold on to that eagerness. As long as you can."

The rest of that evening, and for hours on Friday night, Brendan sat at the desk in his study, organizing his thoughts, getting them down on paper. Thoughts about health care. Drug treatment. Nutrition programs. And—closest to his heart—ways to put an end to racial profiling.

As he wrote, he found his enthusiasm growing. He *could* make a difference. He could talk with people, explain to them, reason with them, help them see. His knowledge, his experience, could be of real value in making some important decisions.

In the beginning, he'd felt railroaded. Now he believed he had a mission.

On Saturday, a bright steamy July morning, Brendan, Sandra, and his parents gathered, promptly at eight thirty, in the breakfast room at the senator's house. The large windows looking out onto the garden were closed tight. Cold blasts came out of the air-conditioning ducts high up.

"Sit, sit," said the senator. "We've got lots to do here."

Josie served coffee, orange juice, and pastries and then disappeared. Pauline took a Danish and passed the plate to Sandra.

"I just can't tell you how excited I am by all of this," said Sandra, as she took a muffin and passed the plate on to the senator. "Just imagine! A chance to get out of here at last. Live somewhere interesting for a change. Is it true—what Deirdre tells me? Is the social life really that glamorous and sophisticated?"

Pauline laughed.

"That's a matter of opinion," she said. "Something you'll have to decide for yourself. But I can assure you it is certainly constant. For many of us, at any rate. Sometimes three or four weeks go by when Stanley and I don't spend one night at home alone. We're either out or having people in."

Dear God, thought Brendan.

"Surely you enjoy it," said Sandra. "You must."

"Of course we do," said Pauline. "Who wouldn't? Being so frequently in the company of the best and brightest in the entire country? Well, the entire world, when you throw in the embassy functions. State dinners at the White House. Sooner or later, you meet everyone who matters. Everyone."

"Sounds like heaven to me," said Sandra.

"Yes," said Pauline. "I imagine it does." She smiled, reached over, and patted Sandra's hand. "Of all the people I know, you're the one I'd say is most likely to fit right in with the life there. No question about it."

"Why, thank you, Pauline," said Sandra. "I'm flattered."

Pauline smiled again.

"How is Jock?" asked Brendan. "Does anyone know?"

"A little better," said Pauline. "Not much. He'll be in the hospital a few more days, and then physical therapy of some kind, I would imagine."

"Please tell him I asked about him."

"We will," said the Senator. He nodded. "So. Strategy for Brendan's campaign."

Pragmatic as always, thought Brendan. *Business first, last, and in between.*

"What we need to do," said the senator, leaning back in his chair, "starting right away and throughout the campaign, is to capitalize on Jock's popularity in this district. Reinforce the positions he's staked out and had so much success with."

"Such as?" asked Brendan.

"Pro-life, most of all. That's what rouses the troops in these parts, more than anything. Nails down the conservative Christians, the Catholics, the people who *count* around here. Don't forget—you've got a decided advantage there, son. A doctor speaking out against abortion. Very powerful point of view in that crucial debate."

"And education, of course," said Pauline. She put her Danish back down on her plate and wiped her mouth with her napkin. "Your opinions would resonate there as well, Brendan—a parent with two children in elementary school. You can speak with authority in favor of accountability and school vouchers, and prayer in the schools. *Very* important to this constituency. We'll need to work up positions supporting the privatizing of Social Security. Strengthening our national defense. What else, Stanley?"

"Well! The thing Brendan is most ideally suited to discuss—health care. We'll want to give a strong endorsement to the plans our Republican leadership is promoting."

"Which are?" asked Brendan.

"A series of prudent adjustments to the system we've got. Carefully thought out, incremental steps that—"

"Ignore the real problems," said Brendan.

The senator's head snapped up. He set his coffee cup down, hard, and stared at Brendan.

"I beg your pardon?" he said.

Brendan reached into his briefcase and took out a stack of papers.

"I have some ideas of my own here. Things I'd like to propose. Some changes in health care among them that are what *I* believe we need."

The senator leaned forward and narrowed his eyes.

"Changes? Like what?"

"Expanded access, most of all. Much more funding for community clinics, which are in desperate need of help. Finding ways to get the insurance companies off the backs of the doctors, who—"

"Hold it!" said the senator. "Hold it, hold it, hold it. We've barely gotten started, and you're already talking about violating one of the sacred rules of politics—never antagonize your base. Those loyalists you can absolutely count on. Reach out, in a reasonable way, to other voters—sure. But keep your base intact. Expand access to health care?" He shook his head. "We've only just managed, after years of effort, to rid the country of the burden of welfare. The last thing anyone wants now is subsidized medicine for those very same people.

"The insurance companies you dismiss so cavalierly? Some of our most generous contributors. There's no way we want to upset them. No, son. These 'proposals' of yours just show how little you understand of what politics is all about. The give and take of it. That's why this kind of discussion is so essential before we let you start talking to the press."

"*Let* me."

"You'll be better off sitting here today listening, son. You leave the strategy—and the issues—to your mother and me. We'll win this thing for you, if you'll just not interfere."

Brendan felt irritation rising inside him.

"No, Father," he said. "I'll be happy to listen to what you and Mother have to say about most things. Education, or foreign policy, or international trade. But not medicine. Not health care. I know what I believe about that. It's what I do. You two have theories. I have experience."

"What you have is a very narrow view," said the senator. "Your experience has been limited to a certain group of patients, with a certain group of ills. Whereas I have spent years—more years than you've been practicing medicine, I can tell you—looking at the broad picture."

"Thereby losing sight of what really matters. The people involved. The daily struggles they go through. I've been there, Father. I've seen it. You can't begin to imagine what it's like."

The senator sighed. "C'mon, son. Don't go all sentimental on me. Not at a time like this. We've got too much at stake here."

Brendan took a deep breath. His irritation was turning quickly to anger.

"Sentimental?" he said. "Well. I seem to have misunderstood my role in all of this."

The senator wagged his head and clicked his tongue. "What's to misunderstand? Your role is perfectly clear—to do what it takes to win this election, this very important election, for our party. For *me*."

"And what I care about is immaterial? The things I've seen and know about don't matter? I'm supposed to just sit back and go along? Sorry, Father. If that's what you're saying, then you've got the wrong man. Maybe we'd better reconsider."

Brendan put his papers back into his briefcase. Sandra was glaring across at him.

"Now, now," said Pauline, in her most soothing tone. "Of course what you care about matters. And you'll have a chance to fight for those things later on. But in order to do that, you first have to get elected." She smiled at him. "You need to trust us to do that for you, son. We're the ones who know how."

That's the problem, thought Brendan. *I don't trust you.*

"Surely you see," Pauline continued, "that you and your father are concerned about the same things. Of course you are. You're just coming at them from different directions, that's all."

"Are we?" asked Brendan. "I wonder."

The senator held up his hand.

"We don't seem to be getting anywhere with this conversation," he said. "I suggest we leave these areas of disagreement behind—for now. We can smooth them out some other time. Let's move on to something that, I regret to say, has become unavoidable in recent years. For any candidate. Something you'll appreciate, though, Brendan. It's what you might call preventive medicine. Inoculation, in a way. What about skeletons in your closet? Things we don't know about. Traffic tickets. Disgruntled patients. Whatever. Best nowadays to get them right out into the open. Don't give the opposition— or the press, God forbid—a chance to uncover them for you."

"Really, Stanley," said Pauline, laughing. "This is Brendan we're talking about, remember? We'll have to invent something a bit . . . outré that he can admit to. So people won't think he's Little Lord Fauntleroy."

She laughed again.

Skeletons? thought Brendan. He had one, all right. More like an atomic bomb. Thoughts swirled around in his head. His first impulse was to protect himself, try his best to keep it hidden. But if he did, people might find out anyway. Use it to harm Jonathan somehow. Mightn't they? The idea of them together was sure to arouse powerful emotions, so the viciousness that might result could be overwhelming.

The other three were looking at him, waiting. What should he do? Then he saw. Clearly and unmistakably. This was not just a matter of loyalty to the man he loved. It was a way out of this madness.

"No, Mother," he said. "You won't have to invent anything. I've taken care of that myself."

Pauline tilted her head, her brow furrowed.

Go on, he thought. *Burn your bridges. Make it impossible to turn back.* What was it Walt Whitman had said? "I am to see to it that I do not lose you."

Brendan realized that he was smiling.

"It's ironic, when you think about it," he said. "Here we are, making all these great plans, while the thing you fear most is sitting right here in your midst."

"What on earth are you talking about?" his mother asked.

"Me. I'm . . ." He hesitated. Too late. He was determined to do it. "I've fallen in love with another man."

The senator stared, his mouth hanging open. Brendan heard a sharp intake of breath from Sandra. He looked across at her and saw the pain in her eyes.

"I'm sorry," he said to her. "So sorry. I never intended this to happen. Please believe me."

"Jonathan Miles," she said softly.

"Yes. Not just a man. A *black* man."

"Oh, dear lord," said Pauline.

Sandra looked stricken.

"I knew it," she said. "Somewhere way down inside me, I knew it. But I just couldn't . . ."

"Imagine it? Nor could I, I assure you."

The senator's face had turned bright red.

"This is the most grotesque piece of lunacy I've ever heard of," he said. "In love with a man! A black man at that." He seemed to flinch. "How *dare* you do such a stupid, vulgar thing to me? Putting everything I've worked for—dreamed of for so long—in jeopardy like this. Have you no self-control?"

"Stanley!" said Pauline.

He glanced at her, then stared out the window. No one moved. Brendan watched as his father calmed himself down, pulled himself together.

"You're right, my dear," he said. "As usual. All of that is for another time." He looked over at Brendan. "And I will have *plenty* to say on the subject, young man, you can be sure of that. But right now, we have more important things to consider." He cleared his throat. "Just . . . how long has this been going on?"

"About six months," said Brendan. "Since the spring."

"How many people know about it?"

" 'It'? The fact that I love him?" A little sound from Sandra. Almost a cry, but not quite. Brendan turned to look at her again. What could he do? Just press on. He looked back at his father. "No one outside this room, so far as I know. I certainly haven't told anyone. Until now. But . . . that he and I are friends? Have been spending time together? Quite a few."

"Where is this man now?"

"San Francisco. He moved out there last month."

"That far away." The senator nodded. "Splendid. Couldn't be better. I . . ." His eyes narrowed, and the corners of his mouth turned downward. "I want to be sure you know how bitterly disappointed I am in you, Brendan. Horrified, as a matter of fact. But, as I said, we can deal with that later on. Right now, with this election coming right at us, I'm afraid it's got to be first things first. We need to set our personal emotions aside, for the time being"—he turned to look at Sandra—"in the pursuit of a greater good."

He turned back to Brendan.

"Let's put our heads together and figure out the best way to contain the damage. We can get to this . . . person, as quickly as possible. See that he says the right things. If he keeps quiet, everything else is just speculation. It won't even come up, if we play our cards right."

"No!" said Brendan.

Pragmatism—even here, he thought. He was disgusted.

"You stay away from Jonathan," he said. "The worst thing about all of this has been having to lie. I won't ask him to lie anymore."

"Don't be ridiculous, Brendan," said Pauline. "It's a small thing to ask—for something as important as this."

Sandra slapped the table.

"Stop it!" she said. All three heads swung to look at her. Her eyes were full of tears. "Just stop this! My life is falling apart here, and you keep rattling on about this damn campaign. Containing the damage, for God's sake. What about the damage to *me?*"

Brendan felt the full weight of her sadness. Of what he now knew her future would be. A future without him.

"You're right, Sandra," he said. "You're absolutely right. That's what's really important. How you and I are going to get through this. Let's go somewhere and talk about it. Just the two of us."

She tried to smile, but couldn't manage it.

"Thanks, Brendan," she said. "I was feeling so . . ."

"I know . . . I know."

He went around the table, leaned down, and kissed her cheek.

"Let's go," he said.

"Wait just a minute," said the senator. "We're not finished here. I can still fix this. Make sure everything comes out the way we want it to."

"I'm sure you can," said Brendan. "I haven't a doubt in the world. But I don't want you to."

"Stop being so headstrong, son. Listen to me. This is what's best for you. No two ways about it. You can't throw it away like this. So you made a foolish mistake. We all do, at one time or another. It's a shock to me, I have to say. Quite a shock. But it's not the end of the world. We'll just have to work a little harder—and be very, very careful—to see that it all turns out right in the end."

"You're not listening," said Brendan. "Let me try one more time. If it were possible to do this my way, I might consider it. But I'm not going to do it your way. I want nothing to do with that."

"Then you are a fool," said the senator.

"That may well be," said Brendan. "But at least I'll be my own fool."

He looked over at his mother. She turned her head away. He put his hand on Sandra's shoulder. She glanced up and nodded.

"We'll be leaving now," he said. "We need to find a way to sort all of this out. But before I go, I want to tell you how grateful I am to you, Father. If it hadn't been for you and this obsession of yours, I might have missed out on something extraordinary. You see . . . it never occurred to me that I could actually have a life of my own. Do the things *I* care most about doing. That's something you and Mother have never questioned. Have just assumed was your God-given right." He shook his head. "Somehow all that escaped me entirely. Until now."

He smiled.

"Jonathan tried to tell me, but I wasn't listening carefully enough. Now you, Father, in your own blundering way, have managed to jolt me out of my complacency. You've forced me to see, and I can never thank you enough for that."

ABOUT THE AUTHOR

Robert Taylor is the author of *The Innocent, All We Have Is Now,* and *Revelation and Other Stories.* His short stories have appeared in *The Peninsula Review* and *Puckerbrush Review.* He and his partner of twenty-one years, Ted Nowick, recently moved from Blue Hill, Maine, to Oberlin, Ohio.